CITY OF DREAMS

The Second Egyptian Mystery

ANTON GILL

BLOOMSBURY

First published in Great Britain 1993
This edition published 1994

Copyright © 1993 by Anton Gill

The moral right of the author has been asserted

Bloomsbury Publishing Ltd, 2 Soho Square, London W1V 5DE

A CIP catalogue record for this book
is available from the British Library

ISBN 0 7475 1754 1

10 9 8 7 6 5 4 3 2 1

Typeset by Hewer Text Composition Services, Edinburgh
Printed in Great Britain by Cox & Wyman Ltd, Reading

for Stephen Warren

AUTHOR'S NOTE

The historical background to the story which follows is broadly correct, but the majority of the characters are fictional. We know a good deal about ancient Egypt because its inhabitants were highly developed, literate, and had a sense of history; even so, experts estimate that in the 200 years since the science of Egyptology began, only twenty-five per cent of what could be known has been revealed, and there is still much disagreement about certain dates and events amongst scholars. However, I do apologise to Egyptologists and purists, who may read this and take exception to such unscholarly conduct, for the occasional freedoms I have allowed myself.

THE BACKGROUND TO HUY'S EGYPT

The nine years of the reign of the young pharaoh Tutankhamun, 1361–1352 BC, were troubled ones for Egypt. They came at the end of the Eighteenth Dynasty, the most glorious of all the thirty dynasties of the empire. Tutankhamun's predecessors had been mainly illustrious warrior kings, who created a new empire and consolidated the old; but just before him a strange, visionary pharaoh had occupied the throne: Akhenaten. He had thrown out all the old gods and replaced them with one, the Aten, who had his being in the life-giving sunlight. Akhenaten was the world's first recorded philosopher and the inventor of monotheism. In the seventeen years of his reign he made enormous changes in the way his country thought and was run; but in the process he lost the whole of the northern empire (modern Palestine and Syria), and brought the country to the brink of ruin. Now, powerful enemies were thronging on the northern and eastern frontiers.

Akhenaten's religious reforms had driven doubt into the minds of his people after generations of unchanged certainty which went back to before the building of the pyramids one thousand years earlier, and although the empire itself, already over 1,500 years old at the time of these stories, had been through bad times before, Egypt now entered a short dark age. Akhenaten had not been popular with the priest-administrators of the old religion, whose power he took away, or with ordinary people, who saw him as a defiler of their long-held beliefs, especially in the afterlife and the dead. Since his death in 1362 BC, the new capital city he had built for himself (Akhetaten – the City of the Horizon), quickly fell into ruin as power reverted to Thebes (the Southern Capital; the northern seat of government was at Memphis). Akhenaten's name was cut from every monument, and people were not even allowed to speak it.

Akhenaten died without a direct heir, and the short reigns of the three kings who succeeded him, of which Tutankhamun's was the second and by far the longest, were fraught with uncertainty. During this time the pharaohs themselves had their power curbed and controlled by Horemheb, formerly Commander-in-Chief of Akhenaten's army, but now bent on fulfilling his own ambition to restore the empire and the old religion, and to become pharaoh himself – he did so finally in 1348 BC and reigned for twenty-eight years, the last king of the Eighteenth Dynasty, marrying Akhenaten's sister-in-law to reinforce his claim to the throne.

Egypt was to rally under Horemheb, and early in the Nineteenth Dynasty it achieved one last glorious peak under Rameses II. It was by far the most powerful and the wealthiest country in the known world, rich in gold, copper and precious stones. Trade was carried out the length of the Nile from the coast to Nubia, and on the Mediterranean (the Great Green), and the Red Sea as far as Punt (Somaliland). But it was a narrow strip of a country, clinging to the banks of the Nile and hemmed in to the east and west by deserts, and governed by three seasons: spring, *shemu*, was the time of drought, from February to May; summer, *akhet*, was the time of the Nile flood, from June to October; and autumn, *peret*, was the time of coming forth, when the crops grew. The ancient Egyptians lived closer to the seasons than we do. They also believed that the heart was the centre of thought.

The decade in which the stories take place – a minute period of ancient Egypt's 3,000-year history – was nevertheless a crucial one for the country. It was becoming aware of the world beyond its frontiers, and of the possibility that it, too, might one day be conquered and come to an end. It was a time of uncertainty, questioning, intrigue and violence. A distant mirror in which we can see something of ourselves.

The ancient Egyptians worshipped a great number of gods.

Some of them were restricted to cities or localities, while others waxed and waned in importance with time. Certain gods were duplications of the same 'idea'. Here are some of the most important, as they appear in the stories:

AMUN   The chief god of the Southern Capital, Thebes. Represented as a man, and associated with the supreme sun god, Ra. Animals dedicated to him were the ram and the goose.

ANUBIS The jackal god of embalming.

ATEN   The god of the sun's energy, represented as the sun's disk whose rays end in protecting hands.

BES   A dwarf god, part lion. Protector of the hearth.

GEB   The earth god, represented as a man.

HAPY   The god of the Nile.

HATHOR The cow goddess; the suckler of the king.

HORUS   The hawk god, son of Osiris and Isis, and therefore a member of the most important trinity in ancient Egyptian theology.

ISIS   The divine mother.

KHONS   The god of the moon; son of Amun.

MAAT   The goddess of truth.

MIN   The god of human fertility.

MUT   Wife of Amun, originally a vulture goddess. The vulture was the animal of Upper (southern) Egypt. Lower (northern) Egypt was represented by the cobra.

OSIRIS The god of the underworld. The afterlife was of central importance to the thinking of the ancient Egyptians.

RA   The great god of the sun.

SET   The god of storms and violence; brother and murderer of Osiris. Very roughly equivalent to Satan.

SOBEK   The crocodile god.

THOTH   The ibis-headed god of writing. His associated animal was the baboon.

PRINCIPAL CHARACTERS OF *CITY OF DREAMS*

(in order of appearance)

Fictional characters are in capitals, historical characters in lower case.

SURERE:	Former district governor
Akhenaten:	Pharaoh, 1379–1362 BC
AMENENOPET:	Lover of Surere
Tutankhamun:	Pharaoh, 1361–1352 BC
KHAEMHET:	Stonemason
HUY:	Former scribe
MERYMOSE:	Medjay captain
TAHEB:	Businesswoman
NUBENEHEM:	Brothel keeper
Horemheb:	Regent
IRITNEFERT:	Victim
IPUKY:	Her father, Controller of the Silver Mines
PAHERI:	His son
MENNA:	His son
RENI:	Senior scribe, father of Neferukhebit, Nephthys and Nebamun
KENAMUN:	Priest-administrator
NEFERUKHEBIT:	Victim
MERTSEGER:	Victim
NEPHTHYS:	Daughter of Reni
NEBAMUN:	Son of Reni
ANKHU:	Son of Reni
ISIS:	Prostitute

ONE

The end of the knout hit the base of his spine with a force that burst a star of pain through his body, to his fingertips, feet, and skull. The prisoners' heads were shaved but they were allowed no covering as they worked in the granite quarry in the heat of the day. The priests had decreed that the god Ra must also participate in their punishment.

Another blow flung him on to the harsh ground, where the broken rocks stabbed at knees and elbows. Still, he scrambled forward to escape a third lash. He heard the hiss of the scourge through the air, but this time the guard only succeeded in catching him across the back of the legs, where the muscles, hardened by eighteen months' labour, were equal to withstanding its force. But he had no strength left to evade a fourth attack, and lay prone, feeling the sun's harsh heat, tasting salt from the blood on his lips as it mingled with the scented dust of the quarry. A spiked rock close to his eyes loomed large as a mountain.

Summoning the last of his strength he braced himself for another blow. To get more courage he whispered in his heart his name: Surere. From the corner of his eye, he saw the end of the whip flick past. Beyond it, the dirty feet of other prisoners, who were standing out of range, watching.

The guard relented.

'Get up,' Surere heard far above him.

Cautiously, he pushed himself on to hands and knees, fearing that the guard would change his mind; but he looked up and saw the man's muscular back as he walked off, looking for another shirker.

He rose, firing silent curses. The one thing that had preserved

1

his sanity in this southern hell, the Number Seven Red Granite Quarry near the River's First Cataract, was the maintenance of his dignity. He had been a district governor under the old king, Akhenaten, and a district governor he would remain, though it was already long since he had been stripped of rank and title, and shipped down from the City of the Horizon in a convict barge with many of his fellow-officials during the purges that followed Akhenaten's death and the collapse of his new capital.

How long had it been? Two years? Three? Surere had struggled to keep a note of time, but only the annual inundation of the river marked it in the changeless succession of sunny days, at a place where not even the great festivals were noticed. In the time that had passed, most of his former colleagues, senior scribes and civil servants like himself, had perished through the unaccustomed hard labour.

Surere put his survival down to the strict continuation of his inner life. He would never be impolite, nor allow the brutalising effects of the labour camp to enter his soul; though the effort this cost was great. He had known men of culture here who had become so obsessed with self-comfort that they masturbated ceaselessly, their hands straying to limp penises even at work, whenever the guards' attention was not on them, their skin grey, drawn across their faces like papyrus, their eyes milky at the death of intelligence. He had known officials who at the court of the City of the Horizon would never have been seen even by their concubines, let alone their wives, without make-up or unperfumed, now careless even of washing, their ragged loincloths daubed with the crust of faeces, the disgusting stubble of beards on their chins, their breaths foul from neglected teeth and the sour-bread-and-onion doled out to them here.

He fell to work again at the relatively easy task which good behaviour and an ability to survive had earned him: scraping away the chippings that accumulated as the masons worked at cutting an obelisk out of a sloping bank of granite. The palm-rope shackles around his feet still chafed at the worn skin, though by now his feet had grown sufficiently hard not be be unduly worried by them. Diseased feet spelt death for a prisoner. Unable to walk, he was unable to earn his keep, and as no doctors worked in the camp, the end would come either through the blows of the guards, or be sought by the prisoner himself, who might drag himself to the water's edge at night and give himself up to the River.

He gathered dusty shards into his tattered apron, looking down at his calloused hands as if they belonged to a stranger. He remembered touching his dear lover with them. Amenenopet, that sweet boy. He only dwelt on the tender thought for a moment. The purity of youth. How beautiful life would be if one could be spared the disillusion of experience.

Shaking his head, Surere clambered out of the trench to dump the shards on to the waste-sledge which would later be rolled down the slope to the dump. He knew that here in the labour camp one of the many ways to madness led through remembering a happier past.

He turned his heart in another direction. For weeks now he had been cultivating one of the masons. They were semi-skilled men who roughly hewed out the obelisks from the rock before they were loaded on to barges bound downriver for the Northern and Southern Capitals, where master masons would trim them to their final shape, and metalworkers and carvers would adorn them with the hieroglyphs appropriate to the subject of their commemoration.

This man, Khaemhet, would soon be taking a new obelisk to the Southern Capital, and Surere felt confident that at last he would be selected to be one of the very few privileged prisoners to accompany it, though until now no former official of Akhenaten's court among the camp's inmates had been accorded such a favour. The late pharaoh, whose visionary reign had ended so disastrously for the empire of the Black Land, had even been deprived of his name. Now, under the pharaoh Tutankhamun, his predecessor could only be referred to by the words Great Criminal. Surere shuddered. To take a man's name away, even if he were a god like the pharaoh, was to destroy his soul. The thought of non-existence after death was too horrible to contemplate.

The day was well advanced, and the sun, in his *seqtet* boat, had begun the descent to the western horizon. Still the heat beat down, and reflected back from the smooth granite slope, setting up a fierce glow in Surere's face. For a moment he allowed his heart to wander again through the streets of the City of the Horizon, the capital Akhenaten had built as the centre for his new religion, for which all the old gods had been swept away. The pharaoh had taught his people to worship the life that came from Aten – the power that dances in the sunlight. Unbidden, lines from the king's great song came to Surere, and the dust and heat of the labour camp receded. It was as if a cool hand had been placed on his brow, soothing his loneliness and his desperation.

Thy dawning is beautiful in the horizon of heaven,
O living Aten, beginning of life!
When thou risest in the eastern horizon of heaven,
Thou fillest every land with thy beauty;
For thou art beautiful, great, glittering, high over the
   earth;
Thy rays, they encompass the lands, even all thou hast
   made.
Thou art Ra, and thou hast carried them all away captive;
Thou bindest them by thy love.
Though thou art afar, thy rays are on earth;
Though thou art on high, thy footprints are the day.

He stooped to gather more chips of stone, flying from the bronze chisel of the mason. Passing close to the man, Surere could smell his sweat, and thought how it would have offended him once. Now, he was sure, he smelt far worse himself. Sensing his eyes, the mason turned round to glare. Surere straightened up, easing his back, and carried another apron-load to the sledge.

His attention was attracted to the River far below, where a massive barge was manoeuvring itself into position. It must have come down to the quay while he was working, for he had not noticed it before. From its vast beam and length, and its battered appearance, he knew it to be an obelisk barge, and his pulse quickened. Was it possible that this

4

time he might be on it when it sailed, instead of just watching it go?

Controlling his excitement, knowing that hope followed by disappointment was a destroyer here, he worked on for the rest of that afternoon with a diligence which surprised the mason, who put it down to the beating Surere had taken from the guard. The mason speeded up his own work; this was the last obelisk he would have to cut here, he thanked the gods. As soon as it was released from its rocky bed, his indenture would be finished, and he would make the long journey north to work in the limestone quarries of Tura, where no prisoner labour was employed. The mason disliked working with convicts. Their presence, and the smell of their despair, depressed him, made him feel like one of them.

Later, in the compound, on the narrow strip of hard land between the quarry and the River, Surere squatted a little apart from his fellow inmates, stooped over the usual evening meal of *shemshemet*, the glutinous cabbage stew which was their staple diet. There was not much social contact between the prisoners: the authorities had seen to it that few former officials of Akhenaten's court were placed together in the same gangs, and the two Surere shared a tent with at night, along with a dozen ordinary petty criminals serving short sentences for picking pockets or minor fraud, were quiet men, turned inwards, unable to forget what they had been, or face what they were now. Therefore no one minded or noticed that Surere sat apart with his chipped earthenware bowl, spooning the stew into his mouth with his fingers.

Night fell, and here and there a torch – papyrus bundles dipped in bitumen – was lit. Each cast a little pool of light, and stark shadows within it, before giving up to the gigantic darkness. Here, not even cicadas broke the silence, and the only noise, now comforting, now mocking, was the restless murmur of the River.

Against the torchlight, Surere could see the silhouettes of the strong cedar derricks, with their palm-ropes and cradles. Near them, still on the log rollers which had transported it from its birthplace in the quarry to the quay, lay a large mottled obelisk, now just a dark shape, the flickering light making its outline shadowy and threatening. Scooping up the last of his food, he scanned the shoreline for the brawny figure of Khaemhet. There were few people about, picking their way along the shore on some late business or standing in small groups from which the sound of muted conversation came faintly to him. The friendly stonemason was not among them, and Surere reminded himself sternly that he must not let hope get the better of him. Nevertheless, he continued to look until the torches burned low, and there was no one left on the quay except the night guards.

He walked down to the River to wash his eating bowl, and then himself. This was allowed and even approved of by the camp authorities. Security in the compound was relaxed. The quarry and the camp lay on the east bank, and there was nowhere to escape to. Away from the River lay desert. On the opposite bank, if one succeeded in the almost impossible task of swimming the distance, more desert, and the Kharga oasis ten days' march across it. To the south and north, equal difficulties lay. The only way out was by getting on to a barge bound for one of the capital cities, and making an escape from there.

Surere squatted by the dark water. From somewhere out of sight but not far away a girl squealed, her voice quickly muffled. The voice sounded too clear, too innocent to belong to one of the gruff Syrian whores who were kept in a palm-thatched shack, its walls decorated with imaginative pictures of girls strapping their legs around jackasses and baboons, for the benefit of the civilian workers in the camp. Surere thought of Amenenopet again, briefly. What could have happened to him? Sadly, he acknowledged that in his memory the boy's features were becoming blurred. Once, he would never have believed that possible; the thought would have been unbearable. Now, all it elicited was a dry smile. Sentimentality was another road to death.

He stood up, easing his back again, the pain from the beating resolving itself into a dull ache. The moon had risen and its light on the black water made it seem thick, like oil. He started up the slope that led back to the compound

6

and his tent. Halfway up it, he heard the unseen girl cry out again.

The sound made him pause, trying to decide if it had masked another, barely perceived, but which might have been a footfall. He quickened his pace and reached the edge of the compound without seeing anyone or hearing anything more, but before he left the cover of the tall rushes that grew along its River side, a man stepped softly on to the path in front of him.

'Khaemhet.'

The mason looked at him shyly.

'Were you following me?'

'I saw you down by the River. I was going to talk to you tonight but I wanted to be sure to see you alone.'

'There was a girl down there somewhere.'

'One of Kheruef's girls,' said Khaemhet, mentioning the name of the brothel-keeper. 'A new arrival. She came up with a couple of others on the barge this afternoon. Kheruef said he was going to try them out.' Khaemhet took a step closer, then hesitated. 'I didn't want to risk them disturbing us.'

Surere looked at him coolly, smelling the *seshen* with which he had perfumed himself. Khaemhet could not hold his gaze, but looked down at his square, mason's hands, folding and unfolding his fingers.

'Have you news for me?' asked Surere, hardly daring to put the question for fear of a negative answer.

'Yes,' replied Khaemhet.

'And what is it?'

Now the mason's broad young face broke into a smile. Perfect teeth, thought Surere, glad that his own, through hard brushing with the beaten ends of twigs, had survived his imprisonment.

'You can come with me on the barge as part of the hauling crew. The overseer gave permission this afternoon.'

Surere felt such a surge of the god's power through him that he thought he would leave the ground. He made himself breathe slowly and evenly, but he could see that his excitement had communicated itself to Khaemhet, who came closer still – cautiously, even respectfully; but closer, his eyes full of longing. It would be impossible to deny him now.

'Thank you.'

'You have yourself to thank as much as me,' said Khaemhet. 'The overseer thinks you are a model prisoner. It may be that one day you may be pardoned by Nebkheprure Tutankhamun, important as you were in the court of the Great Criminal.'

Surere thought the possibility remote. The boy-king, though wilful, was controlled by two men far more powerful than he was: Horemheb, commander of the army, and of the land in all but name; and the old politician Ay, who had kept his grip on power despite having been Akhenaten's father-in-law.

'When do we leave?' he asked the mason.

'We load the obelisk before dawn. At dusk we leave.'

'And our destination?' Surere's throat felt dry. He could sense a shadow of impatience in Khaemhet at all these questions. The excitement tingled in the air between them. Surere cast his eyes briefly and discreetly down to Khaemhet's kilt to see its cloth, half in shadow, raised by a strong erection.

'The Southern Capital.' Khaemhet took one more step. 'Come. There is a quiet place in the reeds. I have brought good wine.'

'I have forgotten what it tastes like.'

'I have spice-bread and apples too.'

'Real apples? From the north?'

Khaemhet smiled. 'I know what you were used to once.'

Apples were an unheard-of luxury. Khaemhet himself had probably never tasted them, and Surere could not help feeling touched by this mark of respect; but he needed one more question answered before he showed his gratitude.

'When will we be there?'

'In four days. The barge is slow. Now, come.' Surere's wrist was seized by a strong, burning hand, and his vanity regretted his broken fingernails and rough skin.

'I am surprised that you can like me ... as I am,' he murmured.

'You are lovely to me as you are,' said Khaemhet, his eyes soft with desire. 'As you were, painted and scented, with gold on your fingers and toes, you would be too beautiful, and I would be too much in awe of you.'

Surere felt a strong arm round his waist, pulling him into the secrecy of the reeds, and then rough lips and a passionate tongue bruising his own.

Later, as they lay side by side watching a light breeze, herald of the dawn, ruffle the surface of the River, Khaemhet said, 'There is one thing I must ask you to promise me.'

'Yes?'

The mason was embarrassed. 'It is that you must not try to escape. If you do, they will kill me.'

Surere was silent.

'Promise me,' said Khaemhet, rolling on to one elbow to look at his face.

'Of course,' said Surere.

She had gone. He told himself that he had known this would happen; that he had seen the signs; that in any case it had been a dream; but none of that helped. Instead of bowing to the will of whichever minor god it was who dealt with such things as love – perhaps the dwarf-lion, Bes; or Min, with his rearing penis and his whip – Huy felt like a man who has a itch he is unable to scratch; or like one whose scalp burns so much that to tear it off would be a relief. For weeks he had been as restless as a corralled lion. She had gone and she no longer cared. Long before she had told him that she no longer wanted him, her decision had been made. Perhaps weeks, perhaps months earlier, he had ceased to exist for her as a lover. That was the worst. To have gone on dancing so long after the music had stopped.

Now he was chasing a ghost. He thought of writing more letters, he thought of going to her house again. But he knew it would be futile. His only course of action was inaction. He had to accept the most unpalatable truth of all: that the object of your love no longer needs you; you are no longer wanted; your part in the play of that person's life has ended. It was, Huy thought, a searing thing to make your exit gracefully, but there was no alternative. Appeals would be received at best with affectionate embarrassment.

It was the season of drought, *shemu*, and from dawn to dusk all the Black Land endured the dreary, unchanging mildness of the sun. By the end of the year, in midsummer, the heat would be pitiless; but then the River would flood, and restore its green banks. Now was a time of long siestas and – to Huy's frustration – monotonous inactivity.

He had just turned thirty. A year earlier, he had been living alone in a little house in a side street in the collapsing City of the Horizon, contemplating not only the wreck of his marriage but also the ruin of his career. He had been a scribe in the court of Akhenaten, and since that king's fall, no longer allowed to practise his profession but not important enough to punish, he had scraped along as an investigator, a solver of other people's problems. Now he looked around the similar little house in which he presently lived, still alone, in a run-down quarter near the port of the Southern Capital. The one big case he had come close to solving had ended in disaster; and now the single good thing to have come out of it was gone.

He said her name. Aset. He brought her image into his heart and tried to condemn her, but he could not. There had never been any hope of their being together for good; he had known that from the start. The sister of his friend Amotju, and now, after Amotju's death, heiress to half a fortune – the other half, after a protracted legal battle, having been retained by Amotju's widow, Taheb – Aset had never been within his reach, and was as far from it now as the moon.

He tried to push the memory of their last meeting away, but it kept returning to his heart – a painful and unnecessary event, caused only by his having been unable to accept her letter. He wished now, in a spirit of self-torture, that he had not destroyed the papyrus on which her firm hand had spelt out their situation with such merciless exactness. The trouble with the end of an affair, whether it has lasted one year or twenty, Huy reflected for the hundredth time, retracing the barren ground of his life like a dog which has lost the scent, is that the partner who leaves has already left in the heart.

Humiliated and miserable, he had subjected Aset to a series of wretched deaths in his imagination, before regretting each; just as he had envisaged a sudden change in his fortunes, making her accessible to him – but in his thoughts coming at a time when he no longer wanted her, however bitter her penitence might be at having thrust him aside. At his core, though, was a seed which would grow and grow, finally blossoming as the rank flower of acceptance, the harbinger of cure.

By the time Aset had married Neferweben, the former *nomarch* at Hu and now a gold dealer in the Northern Capital, six months after her brother's death and three since her letter of dismissal to Huy, the scribe was beginning to be able to thank his guardian *Ka* for small blessings: that she was no longer living in the same city, and that Neferweben may have been rich, but was also fat and fifty, and missing an ear from a skirmish against desert raiders in his youth. Aset, just turned nineteen, had explained to Huy that she needed to consolidate her fortune and business. For his part Huy, who might have entertained hopes of joining Aset in the shipping business and helping her to expand, in competition with Taheb, her former sister-in-law, now told himself that marriage to such a venal woman would have been doomed from the start in any case. All these new, righteous, male thoughts helped for short periods. In time, however, they had become a poor substitute for an empty bed and no work.

The empty bed could be remedied with ease; living as he did near the port, the whorehouses were close by, and they were maintained to a fairly high standard of cleanliness by the city authorities. But a body paid to be there is no substitute for a heart that wants to be.

Work was another matter. Certain people with influence knew the major part Huy had played in solving the mystery which had ended so tragically; but none of them were friends now. He was tolerated by the authorities, though still kept under occasional surveillance by General Horemheb's police, the Medjays. His ambition – to be allowed to work as a scribe once more – was as far off as ever. Discreetly, he advertised for the work fate had given him. Former colleagues would mention his name as a problem solver at the foot of information papyri, and he made sure that in court and palace circles those whose matrimonial and business interests and difficulties might put them in need of him should not forget his services and his whereabouts. After that, it was a question of sitting, waiting, and growing thinner, together with his dwindling supplies.

Amid shouts of warning and panic from the sailors on the foredeck, the huge barge, sunk to the waterline by the weight of the massive red obelisk in its cradle, wrenched free of the helmsmen's control and, pushed by a vigorous undercurrent of the River, hurled itself against a jetty wall of the Southern Capital. Several men were thrown on to the deck by the impact, and in the brief pandemonium which followed, it seemed as if the boat had split, and might sink, there and then, at the end of its journey. But the groaning timbers held, though a plank in the half-decking astern snapped with a noise like a lightning crack, and one of the derricks on shore swayed dangerously, threatening to fall.

Surere, released from his bonds by Khaemhet, along with the other prisoner-quarrymen brought to augment the crew, cast a quick glance fore and aft. The barge wallowed to such a degree that it was hard to maintain his footing, and river water washed over the deck, making it slippery. Overhead, the obelisk swung in its cradle, as the helmsmen fought to bring the barge under control and sailors threw ropes to those ashore who, catching them, hauled on them in teams in an attempt to wrestle the boat alongside. Taut copper backs glistened in the sun as the huge barge bucked and reared like a living thing.

Khaemhet, standing by the bargemaster at the stern, was looking anxiously from obelisk to quay, shouting orders to men who grabbed stay-ropes and, with long poles, attempted to arrest the great stone's pendulum-like motion. Satisfied that the mason's attention was entirely taken up, and determined not to let this god-given opportunity slip, Surere hurried forward, slipping adroitly between the knots of men, losing himself in the busy crowd of sailors. Finally he stopped and looked over the shoreward side of the barge: it was still swaying away from the jetty wall before crashing into it again, but the amount of swing was smaller, and the movement less violent. If he misjudged his leap and fell, there was still a likelihood that he would be crushed to death; but the chances of that had lessened considerably.

Choosing his moment, he hoisted himself on to the low wooden railing that ran the length of the barge, holding on for balance with both feet and his left hand, and stealing a final cautious look round to see if anyone had noticed him. No one had, but the bustle aboard was abating, and there was less frenzy in the straining figures at ropes ashore. It was now or never. Letting go of the rail with his hand, he pushed with his feet and launched himself forward into space, aiming at a coil of rope near a hardwood bollard.

He landed heavily, grazing knees and wrists on the rope. Rolling over, he quickly found his feet, and walked determinedly, a man on an errand, past and behind the crowd of onlookers which had gathered to gawp and shout advice. No one spared him a second glance: the barge seemed to be under control and the drama had gone out of the moment. Some of the workers ashore had dropped their ropes and crossed to man the derricks.

Brushing the dust from his stained and battered kilt, Surere thanked god that his time in the quarries had made him so fit. Safe in the crowd, he slackened his pace to still the pumping of his heart, and turned to take a final look at the barge. He could see Khaemhet walking forward, though it was too far away to see the expression on his face, and he could not tell whether the mason was already looking for him. It would be as well not to take chances.

There was an open area to cross before he could reach the safety of the tightly-packed yellow and ochre buildings which marked the riverward edge of the town. Noticing a man leading a small procession of three pale grey donkeys, heads and backs bowed under a heavy burden of barley in coarse brown sacks, their shadows long in the late afternoon sun, Surere made himself wait for them to reach him. Once they had, he used them as cover to detach himself from the press of people at the harbour, and headed quickly for the mouth of the nearest street. He did not look back again.

Had Khaemhet missed him by now? A brief sense of regret

at his broken promise was quickly eclipsed by the thought of what would happen to him if he were recaptured, and he moved faster.

Soon he was in the cool gulley of the street. Half running between the windowless walls, he turned a corner and even the sounds of the harbour were shut off. He paused to take his bearings before pressing on, still maintaining the purposeful pace of a man with an appointment to keep. He needed shelter and clean clothes and he needed to get to a part of town where no one would question the arrival of a stranger; where people had their own secrets to keep.

Beyond that his plans were looser than he liked to admit, even to himself. But he was free, and he trusted to Aten, the god of the sunlight and the protector of the innocent, whose power he had never doubted despite all his tribulations since the fall of Akhenaten, to place him in the shelter of his hand now.

TWO

Huy was shown to his place by a dark-skinned girl dressed in nothing but a broad gilded collar studded with oval turquoises and a similar thin girdle resting on her hips. Her breasts were small and firm, the nipples only a shade darker than her skin; because this was a party, she had threaded beads of carnelian into the hair of her pubis.

He drank from the beaker of wine she gave him and glanced around at his fellow guests. Some wore scented garlands round their necks, and most of the women had perfume cones on top of their black wigs. There were fifty people in the pillared hall, in groups of five at small tables dotted around a central area where a quartet of women musicians sat with a singer.

Huy was late, and he gave apologies to the three people at his table – a sad-eyed woman he did not know, her husband, a grain broker whom he knew by sight, and a Medjay captain, Merymose. They were reserved, though no more so than any strangers would be at first acquaintance, and cordial enough for Huy to think that either they did not know his background, or did not care.

'Where is our hostess?' he asked, looking round the room again. The invitation from Taheb had come out of the blue, and at first he had considered not accepting it. He had not seen Amotju's widow since his friend's death, and although the events surrounding it had forced the two of them into an uneasy alliance, she had always given the impression that her feelings for him were anything but warm. For this reason, if for no other, he had decided to attend the dinner party, curiosity having got the better of him. If Taheb had decided to invite him, there must be a reason. He was more intrigued than flattered to notice that he had been shown to a table at which chairs were set, rather than the stools given to the less-honoured guests.

'She will be joining us,' said the broker, indicating the empty chair between Huy and the Medjay. 'She has gone to talk to her steward about the acrobats. They have arrived too early, and have another booking later.'

'I don't see why they can't perform now,' said his wife, who looked bored.

'They would get in the way of the food servers,' answered her husband matter of factly.

'Oh.' She picked up the mandrake fruit by her place and sniffed its sickly-sweet odour, darting a glance at Merymose, who answered it with a friendly look, declining its invitation.

'Don't you think it's a little early for that?' asked the broker, indicating the fruit. Muttering something under her breath, but without venom, the woman put the narcotic down and sighed. The awkwardness of the moment was saved by the arrival of two girls bearing golden plates with honey bread, cucumber, *nabk* berries, falafel and – luxuriously – roast beef. A third carried a pitcher with pomegranate wine, and refilled each beaker. The broker's wife drained hers immediately and held it up for more. The broker pretended not to notice.

In an attempt to deflect attention from this, Merymose asked if anyone had seen the great rough-cut obelisk which had arrived from the First Cataract a week earlier and which had lain on the third jetty ever since, one of the quayside derricks having collapsed during offloading.

'I think they have rolled it on to logs,' said the broker.

'Isn't the quay too narrow for that?' asked Huy, politely.

'The one thing to be thankful for is that the stone didn't fracture,' said the broker. 'That obelisk is to be set up and carved as a memorial to Horemheb's victories in the north during the reign of Nebmare Amenophis.'

'Then it would have been most unfortunate if it had broken,' said Huy, neutrally, avoiding the Medjay's eye. The pharaoh Amenophis III had died over twenty years ago, yet now the carved records on all public buildings were being altered to show that he was the immediate predecessor of Tutankhamun.

16

It would be as if Akhenaten had never existed. And yet during Amenophis's long reign there had been very little military activity. During Akhenaten's reign, when the northern empire had been lost, the commander-in-chief was Horemheb. The fifty-year-old general had now also been elected chief of police, and it seemed that he had the eleven-year-old pharaoh securely tucked into a fold of his blue-and-gold kilt.

'I am surprised that Horemheb isn't having his obelisk sheathed in gold – or at the very least, bronze,' said the broker's wife.

'Why?' asked Huy, though he guessed what was coming. Usually, only obelisks consecrated to the pharaoh or the gods were covered with precious metal. Dazzling in the sun, they were potent symbols of supreme power.

The woman looked at him archly. 'Well, it shows modesty.'

Her husband bit his lip.

'One of the prisoners from the barge escaped in the confusion,' said Merymose. Huy glanced at him, and wondered if he did not see a humorous gleam in his eye. His lean body looked young, but the face belied it; Merymose must have been close to Huy's age, and perhaps older. Huy wondered what his history was.

'Have you caught him?'

'No. It's a problem, too, because he was a political detainee. From the court of the Criminal.' He spoke harshly, and it was clear to Huy that he thought Akhenaten had indeed been a criminal, a betrayer of his country. Huy wondered who the escaped prisoner might be. It was likely that he would know him.

'They're holding the mason responsible in the Southern Prison,' continued Merymose. 'It turns out that he and the prisoner were lovers.'

'What will happen to him?' asked the broker's wife, who had managed to take a pitcher of wine from a serving girl and keep it by her on the table.

The policeman spread his hands. 'If in five days the prisoner is not recaptured, they will cut the throat of the mason.'

'And if they do catch him?'

'Then the prisoner will be impaled, and the mason will lose his nose and his right hand.' Merymose kept his voice neutral, but Huy thought he could detect distaste in it. He looked at him curiously, noticing for the first time bitter lines at the corners of his mouth.

The woman drained her beaker and refilled it. 'Poor people,' she said, turning down her mouth. 'One loses his life for following the wrong leader; the other stands to lose his livelihood and become a beggar at the very least. What a land ours has become.'

'Shut up,' hissed the broker. Merymose looked down, taking a bronze knife to his food. He had certainly heard. The broker's wife, oblivious, ran her foot along Huy's calf under the table and looked at him from under heavy lashes.

'What muscles you have,' she said. 'What do you do?'

The musicians had started to play, the two lautenists and the oboist exploring an undemanding melody against which the fourth player tapped out a gentle rhythm on her tambourine. The singer, for the moment, sat silently. Her turn would come later, as the party became rowdier. Already several of the guests were drunk; one woman across the room had called for the copper bowl and was vomiting into it, assisted by two girls, their faces masks.

Huy saw Taheb before she saw him. She had appeared at the other side of the room, and was now moving from table to table, talking briefly to all her guests, as servants cleared plates, brought further courses, and replaced the melting scent cones on the heads of the women guests. She was dressed in a richly-patterned blue pleated robe which swept in one line from waist to floor. Her eyes, made up with malachite and galena, looked both larger and darker than he remembered. She wore a large collar which reached from her throat to her breasts, made up of alternating rows of lapis and carnelian beads, counterbalanced by a silver *mankhet* pendant which hung down her brown back below the rich darkness of her hair. She no longer wore a wig, Huy noticed; and since he had last seen her, her figure had lost its angular thinness. She moved gracefully across the room towards them, including him in a smile which was truly warm, not just social. Could rediscovered happiness make so much difference, so soon, Huy wondered.

She took fresh garlands from a body servant and came over with them, placing one each around the necks of the broker and his wife, Merymose, and, lastly, Huy.

'I am glad you decided to come,' she said, in a way that told him that she had expected him not to. 'I have often thought of you since we last met.'

'I am glad to see you so well recovered.'

'It has not been so easy. Aset contested the will.'

'What did Amotju write?'

'He left me nothing. Nor the children. It was as if we didn't exist. Half to his sister, and half to his mistress. As she died with him, Aset wanted to take it all.'

'Perhaps she was badly advised.'

Taheb looked at him shrewdly. 'Don't take her part. I know what she was to you, and how she has treated you.'

Huy spread his hands, found himself smiling. 'We all have to look after ourselves.'

'That is true,' said Taheb, not taking her eyes from his. 'Still, Aset is a selfish bitch.'

Huy was saved from replying – if a reply was expected – because the broker's wife had turned grey. She seized the wrist of a passing serving girl. 'Bring me the copper bowl,' she commanded unsteadily.

Course followed course with such disregard for economy that no fish, duck or pork was seen, and the wines of Kharga and Dakhla chased down quantities of beef, goose, mutton and egret. Huy, used to poor man's meat, ate and drank little, and noticed that Merymose and Taheb did the same. As the evening progressed, however, the grain broker became more and more effusive; his wife grew increasingly pale and silent. The acrobats, persuaded to stay, entered and performed after the tables had been cleared, though by that time few paid attention to them.

Huy watched the stars in the broad sky beyond the red-and gold columns of the hall as they grew pale, and as finally with infinite slowness at first, the sky lost its blackness and

19

progressed through every shade of grey to lilac-yellow. He shuddered in the dawn. Taheb had left them to make one more round of the tables; the broker and his wife were asleep.

'Do you want to walk back down with me?' Merymose asked him.

'Certainly.' Huy had no intention of courting a Medjay's friendship, but he knew the value of allies. The captain's expression remained enigmatic – doubtless from professional habit. Nevertheless Huy decided to tell him who he was, hoping that here was a man whom, perhaps, he could trust. It would be a risk because the man was bitter about Akhenaten; but what progress was there without risk?

They were about to rise when Taheb's steward came towards them, a worried expression on his face, leading an equally worried-looking young man, a Medjay constable whose relief when he saw Merymose was apparent.

'What is it?' asked the captain.

'You are needed. I have been sent to collect you. I have horses outside.'

Merymose raised his eyebrows. 'Horses? What has happened?'

'Sir, I cannot make my report in front of all these people.' Half of the guests were drunk, the other half asleep; but the young constable looked at Huy.

The captain turned to him apologetically. 'Let Taheb know that I have left. I am sorry about our walk.'

'Yes.'

'Perhaps there will be another time. I would like to know more about you.'

A warning bell rang in Huy's heart, but he said, 'Taheb knows where to find me.'

Merymose turned abruptly and left, attended by the steward and the policeman. At the table, the broker snored gently. His wife stirred in her sleep and turned to face her husband. Sleep had smoothed the stress from her face and she looked much younger – the pursed lips had softened, and the wrinkles on her forehead and by her eyes had relaxed. There was something childlike and vulnerable about her

20

expression, though the sadness remained, speaking to Huy in the cold dawn.

He wondered what business had taken the Medjay away so urgently. To have sent horses indicated something of importance. The animals were rare, and normally reserved for the use of the royal family, the aristocracy, and the small cavalry units of the army.

'What are you thinking?' Taheb was standing next to him.

'The captain has been called away. I was wondering why.'

'It is a pity.'

'It is intriguing.'

'At least you were able to talk to him.'

'Is that why you invited me?'

Taheb smiled. 'You'd better take care, or your work will have you questioning everything. We don't always act with ulterior motives, you know.'

'I am sorry.'

She laid a hand on his arm. It felt warm, and her touch was positive.

'But I suppose you are right to wonder why I asked you here, after so long.' She paused, weighing her words. 'It is true that I wanted you to meet Merymose. He is an old friend, and a good one. I thought that for you to know one trustworthy man among the Medjays would be helpful.'

Huy looked at her.

'I have done nothing to help you,' Taheb continued, with less than her usual confidence. 'I was not sure how welcome my help would be. Then, after Amotju's death there was so much to arrange.'

Huy remembered that one of the first things she had done was to settle the fee which he had agreed with her husband. He had wanted to refuse it, but necessity had overridden honour.

'There will be another chance to meet Merymose and talk properly. Does he know who I am?'

'I have not told him, but if he is curious he has only to consult the records.'

'There is no reason for him to suspect that I would be in them.'

21

'He is a good policeman. He does not like the political role Horemheb has cast the Medjays in. What did you tell him you do?'

'That I was in business on my own account. He did not press me.'

'And if he had?'

'Then I think I would have told him the truth. You're a good judge of character, Taheb.'

She squeezed his arm. 'Don't think that the only reason for asking you here was to meet Merymose. Come and see me again.'

The sun was touching the edge of the rooftops as Huy descended to the crowded district where he lived, and although in this dead season fewer people were about than usual, the narrow streets were already beginning to come alive. Walking briskly to clear his head, he decided to make a detour down to the harbour to see the obelisk. The stimulation of the evening before, the brief elevation to the life of the rich, being among people again, had now been replaced by anticlimax. There was no one waiting for him, and no one to care whether he worked or not. That there was no work to do lowered him further. He remembered the last days in the old city, when he had loafed around the decaying port aimlessly killing time. It seemed to him that he had got nowhere since then, but Taheb's invitation, and the meeting with Merymose, had excited his heart: there must have been a reason for this to have happened now: or was Horus simply trying to organise his life for him?

After a week, the obelisk was no longer an object of curiosity. The grain-broker had been right about the log rollers, on which it now rested, but Huy was the only onlooker as a dwarfed group of workmen under an overseer looped a complicated rope harness around the vast hulk. They worked hard and fast, and their task was soon completed. A drover brought up a team of ten oxen, which was attached by yokes to the towing hawsers, and within half an hour, amid cries and the cracking of whips, the great granite shape started to move forward, shunting over the groaning logs with infinite slowness. A fresh team of men gathered the logs from the rear as they became redundant and hurried to place them under the nose of the obelisk as the oxen, their patient heads held low with effort, steadily plodded across the baked earth of the harbour square.

Huy had been joined by a small group of children, pausing on their way to school, who were dividing their curious stares between the oxen and himself – this unusual man who did not appear to have anything to do. Feeling selfconscious, Huy set off across the square in the same direction as the haulage team, soon overtaking it and disappearing into the labyrinth of little streets to the south, in the midst of which he lived. Already the day was growing hot, and the mixed smells of fish and spices, so familiar that he barely noticed them, rose to greet him.

His house, like those of his neighbours in the block, was two-storeyed and narrow-fronted, with an open roof terrace. It had a yard at the back and – a bonus – faced not another row of similar houses, but a small square. At this time of day it was all but deserted as most of the people who lived in the district worked on the River or in the markets, which meant that they were up and gone before dawn. Those who did not had other work – in the brothels or the food houses – which meant that most of them would not rise before noon. Huy, who had succumbed to consolation since Aset left him, knew some of the girls by now.

He paused at the entrance of the square to look across at his house. It seemed forlorn and closed up, and he considered not going in, but turning right and following the narrow street another two hundred paces to where it opened into another square. There, a shabby acacia-wood door under a faded sign which read 'City of Dreams' led to a series of semi-basement rooms. In them, for a price, for a modest *kitë* of silver, you could drink, eat, or make love, at any time. The madam, a forty-year-old Nubian of immense fatness called Nubenehem, had told Huy on his first visit that she was in the business of round-the-clock solace.

But that kind of solace was not much good to Huy any more; he needed something more substantial: a replacement

23

for Aset, not a substitute. He put the idea away and crossed the square to his home.

Reaching behind the cheap tamarisk door he located the stone bolt and found it already released.

On his guard, he pushed the door inward cautiously and descended the three steps which led directly to the whitewashed living room. A glance around told him that everything was in its place. A low table and three chairs formed the principal furniture, together with a built-in raised-brick dais spread with palm matting and a decorated linen sheet for use as a day bed during the afternoon sleep. The images of Bes and Horus looked down undisturbed from their niches.

Huy stood in the centre of the room, straining his ears to catch any sound from upstairs. None came from above the wooden ceiling, but that did not necessarily prove that there was no one there.

Looking quickly at the steps which led up to the two bedrooms, he moved stealthily past them towards the curtained doorway at the back of the room which led to the kitchen and bathroom beyond. In neither was there any sign of disturbance, though it was clear that both had been used. The limestone washing slab in the bathroom was wet, as was its low surrounding wall. The red pottery water vessels were empty, and a rough linen towel, though neatly folded, had clearly been used. In the kitchen, a crust of herb bread lay on a wooden platter next to an empty beaker which had contained red beer.

Huy was about to check the back yard of the house when a slight sound coming from the living room made him freeze. Someone was descending the stairs. He moved quickly along the short corridor which connected the kitchen with the living room and drew the curtain aside.

The man on the stairs stopped where he was and stared at Huy with a look that was half-furtive, half-beseeching. He was forty years old and tall, with a face that at first sight appeared strong, until one noticed the soft chin and the wide lips, the antelope eyes. Because he had never seen him without the long hair of authority, Huy did not recognise him at first. Now that he did, it was with mixed feelings.

'Surere.'

'Yes.' The old administrator and the former scribe greeted each other with cautious friendliness unsure what roles they were to play now that the authority of the former had gone. It seemed that Surere was toying with the idea of once more asserting the rank he had enjoyed in the City of the Horizon, but if he was, he soon abandoned it. He was nothing more than an escaped prisoner, and he knew nothing of where Huy's loyalty lay.

Surere put on a smile. 'I am placing myself at your mercy. I hope my trust is not unfounded.'

'How did you find me?' asked Huy.

The tall man shrugged lightly. 'There was talk in the labour camps that not everyone had been arrested. Minor officials had been let off . . .' He let the words hang in the air, regretting having used them, then hurried on to safer ground. 'And the sailors on the barge knew of a former scribe who had helped break a gang of river pirates. Of course I didn't know who, and they didn't know your name. May I come downstairs?'

'Of course.' Huy relaxed the threatening posture which he had taken up unawares. More confident now, on legs thin as a stick insect's, Surere descended into the room.

'It was truly by the grace of the Aten that the barge I came on docked here,' Surere went on. 'I knew that there could be no better place either to hide or to find help than in the Southern Capital.'

'What will you do?' Huy said.

He did not want him in his house. A difficult man to get on with, Surere had always been one of the most zealous of Akhenaten's officials, and at the same time one of the most blindly devoted. This allegiance had been rewarded by the special favour of the Great Queen, Nefertiti, though his adherence to the teaching of the Aten had been genuine and profound, entirely lacking the political motivation of many of his colleagues. That he was homosexual played no role in Huy's judgment of him, but Surere's sense of his own rightness had made him many enemies, not least because he was always prepared to sacrifice anyone and anything to

25

his plans, firmly believing that the correctness of his actions justified any means.

'I have been hiding out for a week, looking for friends who share the old faith. It is hard to ask the right questions, without arousing suspicion, especially when every day you get more tired, dirty and dishevelled; and when your head is shaved and the Medjays are looking out for an escaped *political*.'

Huy let pass the fact that his own question had gone unanswered. 'Then you are fortunate to have found me.'

Surere gave him a smile calculated to be disarming. 'Some sailors at the harbour who work on the gold barges told me where you live. I do not think they were curious about me, but they seemed to hold you in high regard. I came here last night after dark. As you were not at home, I let myself in and bathed and ate. I knew you would not deny such hospitality to an old ... friend.'

'Still, you took a chance. With my life too. If the Medjays had found you here ...'

Surere bridled, remembering the difference in their ranks, but even as a rebuke rose to his lips he mastered his anger. It had not escaped Huy, however, and the former scribe had noticed something else.

'They brand prisoners. You haven't been branded.'

'They brand criminals. Not *politicals*.'

Huy looked at him, thinking about the stonemason the police would kill in five days' time if Surere were not captured. 'What are your plans?' he asked again.

Surere spread his hands. This typical gesture of ordinary Egyptians was odd in one of Surere's refinement. Perhaps, thought Huy, he has picked up vulgar habits in the prison camps. It was the only explanation, though not one that satisfied him.

'I need clothes,' the man was saying. 'And a wig – a dark, straight one. And I need sandals, and a knife.'

Huy interrupted him. He did not like the imperious tone. That was one thing that had not changed. But still a doubt nagged at him.

'Where will you go? What will you do?' he asked.

Surere looked at him keenly. 'I will make my way to the north-east. There is a sliver of land between the northern shores of the Eastern Sea and the Great Green. I will cross there and continue into the old northern empire.'

Huy looked at him. 'But that area is lost. It is all in the hands of desert raiders now, and the coast is controlled by the rebels, Aziru and Zimrada.'

'They cannot cover the whole land. If necessary I will take my people deep into the Northern Desert and establish a colony there.'

'Your people?'

Surere's dark eyes blazed. 'Yes! Do you imagine that we are the only ones left who hold true to the faith of Aten? Oh, I have noticed that you have images of the old gods in your house, but I cannot imagine that you have reverted to them. You have them here for protection.'

He was only partly right. Huy had never quite freed himself of the old beliefs; Bes the Lion-Dwarf, and Horus the Hawk-Headed, Son of Osiris, had always remained secretly in his heart. Perhaps if he was honest with himself their power over him was growing, as the influence of the Aten waned, and because, not long ago, the Horus amulet he wore round his neck had saved his life.

'Where do you suppose you will find followers? Horemheb has declared the Aten dead.'

Surere sneered. 'A general cannot command gods. Far to the south, where Horemheb cannot reach, the Temple of the Jewel maintains its worship. And to the north, too, there are outposts. Small centres where the true faith remains strong.'

'How do you know?'

'We prisoners get transported from labour camp to labour camp, from quarry to quarry, from oasis to oasis, from mine to mine. News travels with us. They can try to break our resistance; but they will never break our spirit. And there is something else I desire.'

'What is that?'

Surere smiled. 'Revenge.'

'The Aten teaches mercy.'

'The Aten teaches justice. Where there has been betrayal, there must be retribution. But you are right too. And do not worry. I will not act before I have received my instructions.'

Huy looked at the former district governor warily. His face had grown calmer, and his body was relaxed.

'Instructions? From whom?'

Surere met his gaze. 'From God.'

Huy decided to help Surere, though he was unsure of his way in the grey hinterland of religious zeal where the heart is stalked by the beasts of madness. He fed his former master, found fresh clothes for him and, since he wore his own hair himself, paid a visit to the City of Dreams, where he knew no questions would be asked, and persuaded Nubenehem to organise a man's wig for him. The large Nubian showed only a perfunctory interest in the task, as he had hoped, but her price for fast service was high.

'Good enough for a noble? Well, it can't be for you. Anyway, it doesn't look as if you are going bald.'

'How much?'

Nubenehem considered. 'A piece of gold,' she said.

'A whole piece?'

She nodded regretfully but deliberately. 'If you want a good one, and you want it today.'

Huy had wondered whether he should not go to Taheb for help – she had seemed more than friendly the previous evening – but he did not know her as he knew this obese brothel keeper. Taheb was too intelligent not to deduce what a request for a man's wig meant.

Nubenehem's professional incuriosity, on the other hand, was unimpeachable.

'All right,' he said, knowing that to bargain would be futile.

'Come back at dusk,' she said, then added, looking at him directly. 'Make time to stay if you can. Kafy is free tonight. I know you like her – and I can't stop her singing your praises.'

*   *   *

Preoccupied, Huy hurried back up the street to his house, his sandals raising dust. A gaunt cat darted across his path to squeeze itself into the handsbreadth of shadow at the base of a wall as he passed, where it settled, glaring at him with pale eyes, the pupils crocodile slits in the fierce light. He looked up from the animal to see Merymose and three Medjay officers waiting outside his door. Merymose was already looking at him. Somehow he managed not to allow his step to falter, and continued on, neither slackening nor quickening his pace, calculating the time he had to compose himself. It would not take him nearly long enough to cover the thirty paces that separated him from the policemen. People were about, and several cast curious stares at the waiting group; though Huy felt confident that no one had seen or heard Surere in the short time he had been in the house. But Huy had left him sleeping, and nothing would help either of them if the Medjays entered now.

Merymose greeted him neutrally. Huy noted that at least there was no aggression in either his face or his voice, and took brief comfort from that: the captain had not been tipped off. It seemed an eternity since they had parted company – but it had only been at dawn on this same day. The Medjay looked as tired as Huy felt.

'I had not expected to meet you again so soon.'

'Nor I.' Merymose's tone was severe, but perhaps that had more to do with the official nature of the visit than anything else. Huy wondered about the escort, and how soon it would be before he had to open his door to them.

'You did not tell me about your past last night,' continued Merymose.

'I wasn't aware that it was something that interested you,' replied Huy.

'It could have been embarrassing for me to be seen with a former official of the Great Criminal,' continued Merymose. 'Taheb should have warned me.'

'I am sure she thought we would have things to talk about and that is why she placed us together,' said Huy. 'As for me, I have done nothing against the edict which prevents me from

29

working as a scribe. If you have read my records, you will know now that I am kept under supervision for some of the time, and that after all I am a very small splinter in the buttock of the state. I doubt if it notices me at all.'

'Let us hope that is all you are,' said Merymose. 'These men will search your house. It is a matter of routine. The homes of all old servants of the Great Criminal are being searched for any sign of the escaped quarryman-prisoner. My own feeling is that, even if you have helped him, you are far too intelligent to allow a trace of your action to become evident to us.'

'Then why are you here?'

'First let these men do their job.' He indicated the door curtly, the bronze bracelet of office on his wrist glinting dully in the sunshine.

Suddenly aware of a tightening at the base of his sternum, and aware too of the beautiful value of the freedom he was about to lose, Huy opened the door and stood aside. The heat of the sun on his face no longer seemed real. He watched the three policemen file into the house as he might have watched actors. He wondered if he should make the usual offer of bread and beer; but this visit was too stiffly official, and in a moment it would be over. He found himself regretting not getting to know Taheb better, now that the opportunity was there; she might genuinely have helped him. He should have let Surere sink or swim by himself. He should have reported him immediately. Perhaps then he might have been reinstated as a scribe. Perhaps . . .

They stood opposite each other in the street. Huy looked at the familiar scene as if the gods had suddenly placed an invisible screen between it and himself. Half an hour earlier he had belonged here, had had his place, had been the object of no particular attention. He longed to be left alone with the simple problems of loneliness and unemployment again – the two pebbles that had seemed like boulders. The gaunt cat loped by. He looked at it and could not believe that it was the same animal he had seen minutes earlier. The truth was that he was not the same person. How could such an upheaval happen to him, and his surroundings not change?

THREE

The girl was not more than fourteen. She lay on her back on a wooden trestle table which stood under a palm leaf awning in the shady corner of a broad courtyard in the Place of Healing. They had placed linen wadding soaked in water around her to keep her body cool, but despite the attentions of the attendants there was no stopping the persistent flies, and although it was still early enough in the season of *shemu* for the sun's heat to be mild, her face was already puffy.

Huy could see no mark on the body to indicate how she had died. She was naked, except for golden anklets and bracelets set with emeralds. A rich girl, then; but he could see that already from the delicacy of her skin, and the fine soft hands which lay crossed over her small breasts.

'What is this?' he asked Merymose cautiously. The two of them stood side by side by the corpse. From time to time a little breeze, trapped in the courtyard, eddied and gusted in their direction, bringing with it the first hint of the sweet smell of decay.

'It is something I need your help with. Or at least your advice.'

Huy glanced at his companion, but there was nothing in his expression except serious concern. There was not even tension or anxiety. It was as if what had happened did not surprise him.

'But you know my background. It's unlikely that asking my help will be approved by your masters.'

Merymose returned his look. 'For the moment I am in sole charge of this death. In any case, I am not making an official request.'

Huy hesitated. 'It is difficult for me. You cannot forget who I am and what I was. With a political prisoner escaped, all of us who were at the City of the Horizon must come under increased scrutiny.'

'Your house will certainly be watched.'

'And I will be followed. I might lead your men to the fugitive.'

'That is true. But, if you were prepared to be of service to us . . .'

'What makes you think I can be of help?'

'Everything Taheb has told me about you. Don't blame her. She wants to help you; and of course people will employ you to help them solve their problems; but that will not make you popular with the Medjays or with Horemheb.'

'Thank you for the advice. I will be careful.'

Merymose relaxed slightly. 'It is a pity that you are not a Medjay yourself. Our organisation is only efficient at keeping the streets quiet, and then not always. As for what you do – investigation – that is something new. It interests me, but I am one of very few, and I need instruction.'

'It would be a case of one blind man leading another.'

'At least they would be moving along the road. And they might learn to find their way together.'

'They might fall over a cliff together, too.' Huy was put at his most suspicious by the policeman's flattery.

'Are you not curious about this girl? At least look at her. I cannot keep the body later than this evening. It must be handed over to the embalmers then, or it will be too late.'

Huy paused before asking, 'Who was she?'

'Her name was Iritnefert. Her father is Ipuky.'

Huy looked sharply at the Medjay. 'Ipuky – you mean the Controller of the Silver Mines?'

Merymose nodded.

'What happened?' Huy was alarmed. Ipuky was one of the most important men in Tutankhamun's court.

'We don't know. A group of workmen crossing over to the Valley just before dawn found her by the shore.'

'Where were they crossing? Not from the harbour?'

'No, further downriver.'

'Nearer the palace?'

'Yes.'

Huy thought for a moment. Ipuky had a house in the palace compound.

'As soon as they reported it, Ipuky was informed and I was sent for.'

'The horses?'

'Yes.'

Huy looked at the girl again. She had a delicate, innocent face; the cheeks still round with the plumpness of childhood. Someone had closed her eyes, placing white stones on the lids to keep them down. There there was nothing in the cast of her features to suggest that she had been alarmed or frightened at the moment of her death.

'Did anybody take note of how she looked when she was found? Of how she was lying on the ground, for example?'

'The first people to arrive were servants from Ipuky's household, and they took the body there. If I hadn't requested a delay the embalmers would have already covered her in natron.' Merymose looked grim.

'You were brave to make that request. What did they think of it?'

'They were astonished; but Ipuky is an intelligent man, and he wants whoever did this caught. I am sure his wife thought I was in league with Set.' Merymose's face betrayed a flicker of amusement. 'But the murderer must be brought in, or I will have to pay the price.'

'It is a pity you didn't see the girl at the place she died. That might have told us much.'

'I know. I talked to the workmen. The foreman said that the girl was lying on her back, her hands folded, as she is now.'

'Was she dressed?'

'She was naked.'

Huy stepped closer to the body. He had no medical knowledge, and no idea of what to do, what to look for; but the calmness of the body intrigued him. It raised many questions.

35

He touched it softly. The sun had warmed the skin, giving it the illusion of life.

'Are there any marks on her back?'

'None that I noticed.'

Huy looked at the girl's hands again: they were without a blemish. Her heels were grazed. The rest of her skin, over all the visible part of her body, was clear and unbroken. He would need a doctor to tell him if she had been violated, but there was no indication of it, not even a bruise on an arm where a strong hand might have held her. He reached gently behind her head and felt her hair and the back of her neck, detecting no damage. He registered the stiffness in her body as he lowered her head again.

'Well?' asked Merymose.

'I can tell nothing,' Huy said. 'There has been no violence, and there is no way of telling the manner of her death.'

Merymose sighed. 'That is what the doctors say.'

'Have you spoken to Ipuky?'

'They have shut themselves in their house. I will speak to their chief steward before night.'

'What will happen to Iritnefert?'

'Since she can tell us no more, I will give the order for the embalmers to take her.' He paused irresolutely. 'The way this has been done, you might think a god was to blame. Has she been struck down by heaven, do you think?'

'No.'

'If she were not the daughter of such an important family . . .'

'Yes, how much easier it would be. I am sorry I could not help. Perhaps Taheb overestimated my talent.'

'I will speak to you again of this.'

'You know where I am. How much time will they give you?'

'Seventy days. The time that it takes to embalm her and send her to the Fields of Aarru.'

Huy wondered, as he walked away, what Merymose would do if in that short time no killer had been found. Someone would be made to die for the crime; but for all his reservations, Merymose did not strike him as the kind of man who would fall on just anyone in order to present a solution. At least, not until the three months had passed and the knife was poised over his own neck.

His route took him past the City of Dreams. Remembering the wig which now he did not need, he pushed open the door and entered the antechamber which served as a reception area and office. There was no other way out of the building than through here, though the girls may have had a secret exit of their own, and this antechamber was guarded more fiercely by Nubenehem than ever a desert demon guarded its cave.

The large Nubian was discussing something – evidently money – with a client who bent over the desk towards her, his back to Huy. A middle-aged man, well-dressed, but furtive.

'It's too much!' he hissed at the madam.

'For what you want to do, it's a bargain. Take it or leave it.'

He half turned, indecisive, and Huy caught sight of a grey profile, vaguely familiar, but the man turned back to Nubenehem before he could place it.

'All right. But they'd better be good.'

'You'll have a ringside seat.'

The man giggled – a horrible noise – before setting off for the curtain at the back of the room.

'Just a minute.'

'What now?'

'Pay first.'

Cursing under his breath, and still keeping his face averted from Huy, the man threw a handful of small silver bars in front of the fat woman, who scooped them up almost before they had settled on the surface of the table.

'They'll show you where to go inside.'

The man vanished. Only now did Huy approach.

'Who was that?'

'You know better than to ask questions like that. He's too important a client for me to tell you.'

'That's a lot of money he paid.'

37

'What he likes is specialised. We don't usually do it.' The Nubian looked up from the couch where she half lay by a low table on which a number of limestone flakes were scattered. They were covered with calculations.

'The accounts,' she explained, deliberately changing the subject. 'The farmers coming in from outside the city always want to pay in so much emmer, so many hides, so much barley. I tell them to pay in metal, it is easier for me to negotiate, but they always reply that it's too hard for them to get. I'd refuse them admission altogether if I could afford to lose the business.'

'I doubt if you'd go under.'

'Maybe not. But this is still a chore I could do without. If you've come for a session with Kafy, you're out of luck – she's booked for the whole night by one of the priests from the Temple of Khepri. If you've come to collect your wig – '

'I won't need it now.'

'Run off, has he?'

Huy looked at her.

'An order is an order,' continued Nubenehem, unruffled. 'And an order fulfilled has to be paid for – if you want more favours in the future.' She rose heavily, fat cascading over her hips, and crossed the room to a large cupboard set in the wall. Drawing a number of bolts, she opened its door and withdrew from the interior an elderly, moth-eaten wig which she flourished in front of Huy.

'There!'

'It's terrible. It'd walk away by itself if you put it on the floor.'

'You wanted something quickly. This isn't a perukier's, you know.'

'You should be ashamed of yourself, treating a good customer like this.'

'Not such a good customer recently,' retorted Nubenehem, letting herself flop back down on her couch. 'What's happened to you? Min desert you?'

Their conversation was interrupted by the familiar sound of a girl's badly-acted laughter from behind the bead curtain which led to the interior of the brothel, punctuated by the growling of a man who is under the illusion that he is cock of the dunghill. The girl remained unseen, but the man emerged a moment later, his eyes, as they caught Huy's, switching from initial guilt to fraternal collusion as he saw that Huy was someone he did not know. In the dark days of the Southern Capital under Akhenaten, Nubenehem had told him once, a father who had sold his daughter into prostitution sometime later visited the City of Dreams to watch a session: his daughter, whom he had never touched himself, was one of the participants. It seemed that the father had gone straight from the brothel to the River and drowned himself. But there was nothing furtive or guilty about this customer, who radiated well being and contentment.

'Nice little ass, that Hathfertiti; but a bit of a tight squeeze.' He gave Huy a connoisseur's wink.

'It's a pity you've gone off fucking,' continued Nubenehem when the customer had left. 'There was a girl here not long ago, looking for fun, wanting to earn a bit on the side. God knows why. One of the aristos slumming. She was your type, maybe a bit on the young side. But you could smell the mandrake fruit on her across the room. I'll tell you what; I'll give you the wig for a silver *deben*. I'll even throw in some henna for you to tart it up.'

Huy dug into the leather pouch at his side, concealed under a fold of his kilt, and withdrew its contents: a couple of silver *deben* were all it contained.

Leaving the whorehouse with the wig tucked under an arm, he reflected that it was worth at least what he had paid to have Surere off his back. At the same time he found it interesting that prison had made the former district governor more passionate about the cause championed by Akhenaten. The pharaoh had thrown out beliefs held for two thousand years, rejecting them as superstitions, and replaced them all by a single god, whose spirit could not be contained in images, whose love extended to all people, and who lived in the power of the sunlight. In the twelve bright years of the young pharaoh's reign – he had died insane aged twenty-nine, his dream and his country in ruins – a new light had seemed to dance in the souls of men too.

But prison had protected Surere from the truth. Huy himself, who had had to adapt to the new world constructed after Akhenaten's fall by Horemheb, had learnt above all that ideals do not change people. He acknowledged now that the majority of people, the great brown mass of the fieldworkers, had not even been noticed by the visionary pharaoh he had followed with such devotion, let alone been affected by his thinking. In a matter of weeks, not months, the old, disgraced order had reasserted itself. The priests of the old deities had emerged from the desert or from hiding in neglected provincial cities in Shemau and To-mehu, and established themselves again, without difficulty, the people grateful to have the old gods returned to them, who demanded no more than unquestioning duty, propitiation and sacrifice; gods who did not require a man to think for himself; gods who forgave sin if the price was right, and who guaranteed a good time in the Hereafter.

Surere had been unusually inflexible for an intelligent man. Always insisting on the purity of life, on the importance of family existence, he had gone far beyond the mild precepts laid down by his mentor. Before madness overcame him, Akhenaten had at least understood that there would always be a gulf between an ideal and its realisation. The Aten itself was amoral; but in life one should always forgive a man who had sinned. In his province, Huy remembered, Surere had tried to impose what he had interpreted as the supporting columns of a decent society: sexual responsiblity and even monogamy were held to be the roots of a stable family; sexual relations between members of that family were restricted to cousins. Concubines were discouraged. In Surere's province, there had been many transgressions, despite the loss of privilege which was the only punishment he had dared impose, though there were rumours that in some cases he would have preferred to apply the death penalty. There were rumours that in some cases he had.

Even the king, who, unlike his district governor, had practised these precepts himself, had not expected his subjects to do so too, though he hoped they would strive towards the ideal. His own queen, whom Surere had revered so deeply, when she requested that she be buried not in the new City of the Horizon, but near her old home, in the Valley of the Dead across the river from the Southern Capital, had been granted her wish, though it had hurt Akhenaten deeply.

Nefertiti had died young. Five floods at least had fertilised the Black Land since her departure in the Boat of the Night. Since her husband had gone to join her, her tomb had been neglected, and sand was already drifting across its entrance, covering it inexorably in a red blanket. It had been thought among the citizens of the Southern Capital that the new pharaoh, Tutankhamun, whose own Chief Wife was a daughter of Nefertiti, might have renovated the Death Halls of her mother. His neglect of such a sacred duty had scandalised some, even members of the old priesthood, but behind Tutankhamun's inaction the policies of Horemheb were discerned, and no public protest was raised. The king, after all, owned the land, the people, every animal and everything that grew. There was no questioning his word or deed. Even the thought of doing so would not enter the hearts of most.

Huy wondered how Surere would react to the world he found himself in now. He had not visited the Southern Capital, Huy felt sure, for at least eight years, and possibly longer, following the removal of the court to the new City of the Horizon downriver. In that time, its geography had changed little, the only difference being that more and more houses had squeezed themselves on to the mound of detritus that had built up over generations to form the hill on which the city squatted, above the highest level of flood the river could attain.

The man had survived in his pursuit of a political career by mingling adaptability with discretion. But his adaptability did not apply to his tenets, merely to his instinct for self-preservation. An amoral man applying a fixed morality to others might not have hoped for the success Surere had had; but now, with so much ranged against him, in a world so different from the one he had lorded it in, Huy wondered how he would get on. He found himself hoping that the man would succeed in his plan to take a knot of followers remaining

41

faithful to the Aten – if they existed – out to the deserts which, he had heard, extended to the east of the Great Green, and form an outpost of the new religion there.

Huy had lived a more realistic life. He remembered the release he had felt when he had first heard the teachings of Akhenaten, which had cut away the rotten trappings of the old beliefs, festooned as they were with the cynical speculation of the priests. Now, though, having to live again in a world where ideals were something to be discussed by intellectuals and certain priests, but never applied, as they would have got in the way of Horemheb's programme of reform, Huy found his feelings dulled. Unable to accept again the superstitions he had discarded, nevertheless with time and misfortune he found himself turning back to the three deities who had guided his early life, and helped him through his harsh apprenticeship as a scribe: the reasonable Thoth, ibis-headed, god of the scribes; Horus, son of Osiris; and the protector of the hearth, Bes – the little god of his childhood.

As he reached his door he found his thoughts turning once more to the urgent problem of putting food in his belly, and a part of his mind registered with pleasure that these thoughts were at last supplanting the ones in which he alternately pined for Aset and visited unholy vengeance upon her. As for his former wife, Aahmes, she had become a shadowy figure who sent him a letter from the Delta every new year, at the midsummer *opet* festival, with news of his favourite son, Heby. He tried to imagine how the boy would look now that he was nine. In her last letter, Aahmes had spoken of a new marriage. Huy tried to imagine her going through the simple ceremony with someone else, and could not. What seemed most real was that Heby would have a new father – someone who was there, instead of a remote figure several days' sail upriver.

He was grateful to Taheb for having sought work for him through Merymose, and wondered if he had been unduly mistrustful of her. Perhaps she had begun to realise that she had been the victim of an unhappy marriage, rather than simply the cause of one. After her husband's death she had borne herself with a mournful dignity which had done her standing no harm, and taken the funeral food to the tomb herself with a regularity and devotion which would have shamed women lamenting better-loved partners. Now he had met her again, he found a different woman – and the one who was now emerging was the one with whom, ironically, Amotju could have been happy.

Huy entered his house, and its drabness both depressed and reproached him. He scratched together some lentils and *nebes* bread, and found a small jar of black beer and a clay straw to suck it with, thinking of the contrast between last night's dinner and this. After he had eaten he lit a small oil lamp to dispel the gathering gloom, and by its light fought off the silence by indulging in some desultory tidying, which consisted of gathering together assorted scrolls of papyrus and articles of clothing scattered about, and dumping them into two chests – one for each. He dropped the wig into the papyrus-chest, wondering what he would do with it, and whose head it had adorned before Nubenehem had come by it. Thinking of that, he made a mental note to burn it in the morning.

Finally tiredness overcame him and he went out into the yard to fill the water jars for his bath. Then he climbed the steps to his bedroom, stripping off his kilt, and lay down stiffly.

He expected to fall asleep quickly, but his heart would not let him. For no reason that he could think of, the image of Nubenehem's customer, the furtive man in the brothel, came back to him. Why was he familiar? And why was such a well-dressed man using a brothel like the City of Dreams? Huy nagged at the problem until, unable to solve it, he became drowsy. Perhaps after all it was nothing more than that the man reminded him of someone from the old days, and it was not unknown for people from the palace compound to slum in the harbour quarter now and then.

The following morning he awoke refreshed, and the day no longer stretched before him like a void. Not that there was any more purpose in his life than there had been yesterday; but the events of the previous twenty-four hours had shown him that Ra could and would produce the unexpected at the most surprising moment, and he could not suppress the hope that his chance meeting with Merymose might lead somewhere. Huy had been more help to the Medjay than he realised; but it was on his own account that he decided to take up Taheb's invitation and visit her.

He was curious about how she would react – had she just given it out of social politeness, or had she meant it? Also he was interested to find out more about the dead girl and her father, Ipuky. There was no question of his approaching the father directly as a man such as Huy would not be allowed into the palace compound; but Taheb was a rich businesswoman, and if she did not have any personal knowledge of the family, she would have contacts who would.

As he left the house Huy glanced around the square, and along the streets that led from it; but there was no movement at any of the few windows which looked on to the street, and the handful of people about were all familiar to him. He realised that it had been a while now since he had put himself on the lookout for Medjays shadowing him. The ones appointed to do the job had never been very good at it, but he had heard a rumour that Horemheb was training a secret corps of police, answering to him alone but set up in the pharaoh's name and in the interests of national security. It could be that the men and women of this corps were already on the streets and that, army trained, they would be better at surveillance. He thought briefly about Surere again, and wondered with something akin to panic whether he would reappear; then, angered with himself at this disloyalty to a former colleague and certainly a fellow-sufferer under the new regime, he dismissed the matter and concentrated instead on what he would say to Taheb.

He made his way through the twisting streets of the harbour district, crossing the little squares where the market traders were spreading linen sheets on the ground before decking them with neat conical piles of vegetables and spices whose reds, yellows and greens shone out brightly against the white. Against walls, jars of oil, cheap wine, and black and red beer were stacked, and here and there a low table displayed jewellery. Near one of these, a guardian-baboon squatted, on a leash long enough to enable it to run after any would-be shoplifter and seize his thigh in its jaws. The ape gave Huy a baleful stare as he passed, then blinked and yawned, displaying a set of formidable yellow incisors. Nearby, a fisherman was gutting his catch, while his wife, weighing machine in hand, sorted the individual mullet by size. The smell of freshly-fried falafels hung on the air, reminding Huy that he had not yet breakfasted.

Gradually the streets became broader, the squares larger and less crowded with traders. He walked south-eastwards from the River, uphill towards the wealthy residential district where Taheb lived. Tamarisk and acacia trees stood by walls whose whitewash was truly white, not dun coloured, and which hid formal gardens, not cramped courtyards hung with washing. Huy passed fewer people as he penetrated the quarter, and most of them were servants. The occasional curtained litter or rickshaw sheltered its rich occupant from the sun as he or she ventured out on some errand. Nobody paid any attention to Huy. He guessed that, if anything, he must look like an under-steward employed in a moderately well-off family.

That was certainly the impression he gave to Taheb's gate-keeper, a squat man with one wall-eye, who appraised him pessimistically with the other when he asked for the mistress of the house. He was saved by another servant who recognised him from the banquet. Amid apologies, he was ushered in, and led to a familiar inner courtyard to wait.

The courtyard was where he had last seen his friend Amotju. Then, it had been an austere place, with only plain wooden furniture, painted dull red, to relieve the stark whiteness of the walls. Now, Taheb had set it with large earthenware tubs, from which a profusion of tall dark-green plants grew. Two of them bore long fruits like courgettes, though pink in colour and set with needles like a cactus. Two-thirds of the way up the wall a frieze had been painted, depicting the work of the shipping company which Amotju had inherited from his father. There, unmistakably, were the pylons of the port of Peru-nefer, near the Northern Capital. Further along, there was an Eastern Sea

45

ship, beating down under its huge sail along the desert coast on its way south to Punt to collect a cargo of exotica: blackwood so dense it sank in water; the fierce spotted cats which could be tamed to become the pets, or hunting land falcons of the rich; myrrh; the long teeth of the great forest beast. On another wall, the heavier ships which crossed the Great Green on less arduous journeys to Byblos and Kheftyu.

'Do you approve?' a voice behind him said, and he turned to see Taheb, dressed in a pleated robe of light wool, slit for coolness on one side to the top of her brown thigh, and edged in dark blue threaded with gold.

'Yes. You have made many changes.'

'It is important, if you are to continue to live in the same house.'

'Had you considered moving?'

She shrugged. 'I am comfortable here, and there is the office. I bear no ill-will, so there are no ghosts to rise against me.'

Huy spread his hands. 'You invited me, so I came. But I should have sent word.'

She smiled. 'You have chosen a good time. The wind freshened, and the two diorite barges in harbour due to go south sailed early. So – you may command me.' She opened her long arms and let them fall gently to her sides again with another smile, gesturing to a couch and taking a seat herself nearby. As she walked to it, Huy wished that he could see more than the slit in the dress revealed. How could this woman have become so attractive? She had been withered before; now she was in bloom.

'Do you know why Merymose was called away from here so urgently?' he asked, as a body servant brought honey cakes and wine.

Taheb's face became sad. 'Yes. Poor Iritnefert.'

'I want to ask you about her.'

She raised her eyebrows. 'Has Merymose brought you in on his investigation?'

'No – but thank you for the contact.'

She shrugged. 'Your work is interesting, and I think you are good at it. Merymose is an intelligent man. You might learn from each other.'

Huy wanted to ask more about the policeman, but decided that now was not the time. He did not know Taheb well enough to trust her yet.

'Did you know the girl?' He said.

'We knew the family. Occasionally we would be contracted by Ipuky to bring a cargo of silver ingots north from the mines on the Eastern Sea, and then upriver from the Delta. There is an overland trade-route now, so we do less business with them.'

'What sort of man is he?'

Taheb's smile did not slip, but she was immediately guarded. 'How much further is this going?'

'No further than me. I cannot speak to Ipuky myself, though no doubt Merymose will.' He hesitated, and then continued. 'I am interested. That is all. Merymose asked me to look at the body.'

'Poor girl. Was she mutilated?'

Huy looked at her curiously. 'No. She was unblemished. Do you ask that for any reason?'

'I associate murder with violence. I imagined she'd been knifed, violated. You have an inquisitive and suspicious mind.'

'It is getting worse.'

'So, why are you asking me these questions, and why should I answer them?'

'I am asking them to satisfy myself, and because doing nothing bores me. It may be that my help will be called for. If not, I will do nothing with the information you give me. It will be as if this conversation had never taken place.'

'You are diplomatic.' She embraced him with her eyes, pleased, and as she poured them both more wine, rewarded him with a view of her leg. Fine golden hairs, which but for the sunlight on them would have been invisible, shone against the soft brown skin of her thigh. What *had* happened to the old Taheb?

'Ipuky is a civil servant. I am too young to remember but I think he began his career as a supervisor in the turquoise mines of the Northern Desert, towards the end of the reign of Nebmare Amenophis. I know that he was one of the ones who resented the rise of the military. He kept petitioning Amenophis to restrict the granting of golden battle honours – not that the battles were anything more than skirmishes then.'

'Do you know what happened to him during the reign of the Great Criminal?' Huy was grimly amused at how easily he could deny his former master's name.

'You don't have to obey Horemheb's decrees here, and we are not overheard,' said Taheb. She seemed irritated that he had not taken her into his confidence by using Akhenaten's real name. 'The answer to your question is that I don't know. But he was certainly in office – probably still in the mines department – and managed to hang on afterwards. Did you never see him at the City of the Horizon? There were plenty of career administrators and businessmen along with the idealists, you know. And they were just as necessary to Akhenaten – possibly more so.'

'And most of them were forgiven.'

'That should not make you bitter. Of course they were. They were given the chance to recant, they did so, and they went on with their work. They are the ribs and backbone of the Black Land, and the army is its muscle. Without them the heart cannot function, however much it rules them.'

'Can it rule what it cannot control?'

'Yes, as long as it thinks it controls. Akhenaten tried to break that pattern and look what happened.'

'Tell me more about Ipuky's family.'

Taheb considered. 'There were three children. Iritnefert was the only daughter, and she was the youngest. She was unmarried, and there was no one in prospect as far as I know. Her mother divorced Ipuky and went to live in the north of the country with one older son. Paheri. He was already grown, and became a priest of the Aten.'

Huy drew in his breath.

'What is it?' asked Taheb. 'Did you know him?'

'Yes. He was Surere's right-hand man. But I did not know that he was Ipuky's son.'

They were silent for a moment, both thinking of the escaped quarryman-prisoner.

'I wonder what happened to Paheri, after Akhenaten's fall,' said Taheb.

'He disappeared, like so many,' said Huy. 'There would not have been many to mourn him.'

'Except his mother. He always thought that she had been wronged by Ipuky.'

'She must have been the only woman Paheri ever liked. His nickname was Sword of Surere. They may even have been lovers, though they parted company towards the end.'

'What happened?'

'There was a bitter row. Paheri accused Surere of taking too soft a line; but I also heard that he'd found Surere in bed with a stable boy. Surere certainly began to enjoy the fruits of power towards the end, but Paheri was a deeply jealous man.' Huy made a dismissive gesture. 'That is all history, and Paheri must certainly be dead. Where in the north did Ipuky's wife go? I don't think she ever came to the City of the Horizon.'

'She came from Buto originally. I think that is where she lives still. She never remarried.'

'But Ipuky did.'

'Of course. In his position, he had to. I do not know the name of his new Chief Wife, but I think that apart from her, he only maintains concubines. Most people think Ipuky is married to his work. He has the reputation of being a cold man, and appears to enjoy neither his power nor his wealth, though I find that difficult to believe since he works so hard to keep them.'

'Are there children by his second marriage?'

'I do not know them, nor how many there are.'

'How old might they be?'

'Certainly no older than eight. Still children.'

Huy paused, thinking. 'And do you know anything of Ipuky's other son – Paheri's brother?'

49

This time Taheb was evasive. She tried not to show it, but she was not quick enough for Huy. 'I don't know. There was something wrong with him. I think the family managed to find him some kind of posting in a province in the north-west, towards the Land of the Twin Rivers. But no one has heard anything of him since the collapse of the northern empire.'

Huy knew better than to press her, and changed the subject. He already had enough to think about. 'How are your own children?'

She looked at him archly. 'Growing up. I am twenty-five. An old woman.'

'Tell me that again in fifteen years. You will cause many sighs yet.'

'You should have been a courtier.'

'I did try.'

A scribe came into the courtyard timidly, his pen-box swinging from his left shoulder and a sheaf of documents in his hands, stained with red and black ink.

'I am sorry,' he said to Taheb, nodding carefully to Huy and bringing his arm across his chest in greeting. 'These are the shipping lists you asked for. You said they were to be brought as soon as they were drawn up.'

Huy stood up.

'There is no need for you to go,' said Taheb.

'Yes.'

She shrugged, standing too, taking the papers and nodding dismissal at the scribe. She came a little closer to Huy. 'If only I could find you a job here.'

'Long ago I wanted to be a boatman. Now I know I shall never have the skill. I cannot work as a scribe, and I am beginning to enjoy being free. How could I be useful to you?'

Taheb embraced him with her eyes again, but said nothing. Huy could not interpret the nature of that look. 'I must ask you one more question. You knew Iritnefert a little?'

'Yes, a little.'

'What was she like?'

There was a pause before she answered. 'A fire in the wind,' Taheb said.

FOUR

It was a slow process, needing the kind of patience he did not have, but at least Huy was spared the tedium of the cutters, whose sole job was to trim the reeds to a regular length, about the same as a man's forearm. The next step was for the peelers to strip the reeds of their rind, cutting it off with sharp double-bladed knives made of flint. These two tasks completed, the exposed pith was cut into narrow strips like ribbons, which were then placed side by side on a large, perfectly-flat slab of limestone which was kept permanently damp by boys scattering water on it, ever-moving fingers flicking across from earthenware pots.

The slices were perfectly aligned, and then a second layer was placed across them at right angles. Huy's job was to tamp this second layer down on to the first. With two other men he worked his way rhythmically across the sheet, beating the second layer gently with rounded mallets until the starches produced from the pith welded all the strips together to form a sheet, the size of the stone, of white papyrus. Once the process was completed, older boys, apprentice papermakers, came and dislodged the sheet, taking it away to the drying trestles, where it had to be carefully watched and removed after it had dried but before it began to turn yellow in the sun. In another part of the factory, the sheets were glued together to make large rolls, or cut into smaller pieces for letters and shorter documents.

Huy had taken the job after ten days of waiting hopefully for word from Merymose. Then, the emptiness of his purse and the bareness of his kitchen had forced him to find work of any kind. Confronting Nubenehem with his problem, she had introduced him to another customer of the City of Dreams, an elderly papermaster with flaccid skin and a bald pate ringed with long, dank hair. This man, who told Huy that he only went to the place to drink, never having had a problem when it came to finding a girl, was looking urgently for somebody to work on his paperbeating team as one of his men had died suddenly from river fever. Huy knew something about papyrus, having spent most of his life writing on it, and had managed to convince the man that he knew how to make it, without giving away too much of his true background. He had been taken on.

At first, as he worked, he had reminisced pleasantly to himself about the smells and the texture of paper and ink, and about the pleasure of opening a new roll of papyrus, laid out as far as there was need on soft leather spread over a wooden writing desk; then mixing the ink powder with water, and the nervous moment of dipping the brush to make the first signs – to load the brush just *so*, in order that the ink would be absorbed by the paper before it could run down it. He remembered the floggings which, when he was a student, had followed the botching of a papyrus. Now, after thirty days at this backbreaking and endless task, he realised why. But his fellow workers were happy and prosperous. Demand for their product was unceasing, and their labour was steady and safe.

Its dullness stifled Huy's heart, and he began to question the sense of feeding his belly at the expense of his mind, though such noble sentiments could hardly be his to indulge. He thought of Merymose, and wondered how he was progressing, with time running out as the embalmers pressed on with their task. He had not returned to see Taheb, partly out of pride, partly out of uncertainty. At their last meeting a line had been reached, and despite the urgings of his senses at the time, he was not sure that they wanted to cross it. At the same time he was puzzled by her silence, after such friendliness. Was she thinking as he was? Was each of them waiting for the other to make the next move?

Ten more days were to pass before the longed for interruption to Huy's humdrum existence occurred. For some time now he had not been aware of being followed, and he knew, too, that no one had searched his house in his absence. Every day when he left for work, he would leave objects such as a scroll or a limestone flake, or his *kohl*-pot, a certain measured distance from the edge of the table on which they lay, and from each other. However carefully the house might have been searched, those distances would have changed. They never did. Huy put it all down to his regular job. Perhaps the authorities thought that he had finally knuckled under. It occurred to him that a full belly was not all he had his tedious employment to thank for.

One evening, however, as the never-failing north wind freshened, rustling the tops of the *dom* palms as he walked back to the harbour quarter, he had the impression that someone was dogging his steps. To make sure, he altered his usual route, ducking down alleys no wider than a donkey's girth, slipping across little squares where five ways met. The streets of the harbour quarter were quite unlike the regular, broad thoroughfares of the rest of the city. This part of town had grown up organically, defying and outgrowing any order the town planners may once have tried to impose, and Huy knew it intimately. Yet he was unable to shake off his pursuer. Finally he gave up the attempt, and took the most direct way back to his house. He was almost there when he heard the sound of running feet behind him, and turned to see Merymose coming towards him.

'Thank you for the guided tour,' said the Medjay. He looked tired and drawn, but his mouth was still a determined line.

'It was you? I'd have thought you'd have made a better job of it.'

'I wanted you to know someone was following you, so that I could be sure you'd lead me a dance. That was the only way I could check that no one else was on your tail.'

'Why?'

'I'll tell you inside. I shouldn't be here, and I certainly shouldn't be talking to you, but I have no option.'

Once seated in Huy's living room, Merymose relaxed, but only a little, and he could not remain in his chair long, but kept getting up and pacing the narrow space between the front door and the rear wall.

'First of all, I should explain why you heard no more from me after you came to see Iritnefert's body. Somebody must have reported the meeting, because I was summoned to the priest-administrator's room at the palace the next day for a tongue lashing. Something along the lines of loss of professional dignity, enlisting the aid of socially undesirable persons in official business. I was lucky to keep the case.'

'Have you made any progress?'

'I haven't been allowed to move. I wasn't able to talk to Ipuky myself. I wonder if that would have helped. All I have been able to find out is that he was a remote father. After the mother's departure, he lost interest in the girl, turned over her upbringing to one of the house matrons. She was severe, used to have Iritnefert whipped for the slightest misconduct. The girl grew up without love.'

'That is much.'

'That is all. There is no clue to follow. And now I am no longer in charge.'

Huy looked at him. 'Who is?'

'Kenamun.'

Huy knew the man by sight and reputation. In temperament he was not unlike Surere, a career official who had dedicated himself to climbing to the top of the power structure, though he had chosen the priesthood as his channel. He was as inflexible in his allegiance to Amun and the old gods as Surere was to the Aten, and during the reign of Akhenaten he had fled to the oasis of Kharga to escape death. His loyalty had stood him in good stead after the restoration, and he was now a commissioner of police for religious conformity – a post which did not prevent him from working in any other area which Horemheb, through the king, saw fit to appoint him to.

'When did this happen?'

'Yesterday.'

'Do you know why?'

Merymose sighed. 'There has been another killing. They begin to think that it is the work of a demon. But how? There is no violence. Not a mark on the body.'

'Who was she?'

'The youngest daughter of Reni, the Chief Scribe.'

'How old was she?'

'She would have been fourteen at the time of the *Opet* festival.'

Huy looked grim. 'And how was she found?'

'The middle sister found her by the pool in their garden. The family also live in the palace compound. She was naked, laid out with as much care as if Anubis himself had done it.'

'Did you see her yourself?'

'Yes. Reni ordered that the body shouldn't be touched and sent a servant directly to me. I should have reported it first, but I thought I could always plead urgency if I was disciplined again, and I couldn't take the risk of being denied access.'

'Did you talk to Reni?'

'Yes. He's an intelligent man, but his heart was darkened by his daughter's death, and there was nothing he could tell me. His house is large, and his children are old enough to be free, though all still live under his roof. He and his Chief Wife dined alone at sunset, then he went to his office to work. He didn't see any of the children that evening, except the oldest girl, who is eighteen and unmarried, and acts as his secretary. The middle sister discovered the body when she came home at about the sixth hour of night.'

'How many children are there?'

'Two surviving daughters, and two sons.'

'When did he summon you?'

'Soon after. I went immediately, as I said.' Merymose looked troubled. 'I reported the killing as soon as I left them, leaving a man there and asking them to touch nothing; that was about the ninth hour. Then I waited for orders. At about the second hour of day I was told that Kenamun would be leading the investigation. Of both killings.'

'With the same time limit they gave you?'

The Medjay smiled wearily. 'That threat has now been lifted. Even they can see that there must be a connection between the deaths.'

Huy did not reply. He knew Reni well, as he was the only scribe who had held high office both under Akhenaten and the new regime. It was certain that he had bought his freedom by betraying former colleagues. He had been farsighted enough to recant before Akhenaten's death, making a discreet escape from the City of the Horizon by barge at night with his family. Once he had arrived at the Southern Capital, he had proclaimed his loyalty to the old gods loudly and publicly, disowning the Aten and throwing himself on the mercy of the priests of Amun, who even then were growing bold as the revolutionary pharaoh lost his grip both on reality and his empire.

'I read your heart,' said Merymose. 'Do you read mine?'

'The connection is too slender.' But Huy's thoughts raced. The daughters of two high officials, both of whom had survived the change of regime – both of whom, depending on your point of view, could be seen to have betrayed Akhenaten. 'In any case,' he continued, 'I do not see how I can help you. You said yourself that you are taking a risk by meeting me.'

Merymose paused before replying, and when he did so he was awkward. 'I do not know why I even trust you, but I have no men trained to use their hearts in the way you are able to as a gift of Ptah. You seem to know your craft instinctively.'

'Taheb must have been very warm in her praise.'

'I have listened to you twice now myself.' Merymose stood up and made for the door. 'Look out for me first. I will go if no one is there.'

'You cannot make a habit of coming here.'

'I will ask Kenamun if we can engage you – professionally. He is more broad minded than the priest-administrator; and he wants to succeed in this. How much better to engage someone to help who cannot claim official credit for himself when the matter is solved.'

'You give me little encouragement.'

'You will be paid, Huy. In any case, you were not born just to make paper.'

'I don't know what I was born to do. I don't know that it matters.'

'Perhaps your true profession has found you. It is something that happens.'

Huy paused before replying. 'I have a question for you.'

'Yes?'

'What did you do during the Great Criminal's reign?' If he was going to work with Merymose, they both had to reach a position of trust.

Merymose's face hardened, and it was a long time before he answered.

'I was in the garrison at Byblos. When Aziru sent his Khabiris against us, finally, we had been under siege for three years. In that time the Great Criminal sent us not even one reply to our requests for help. We were starving and reduced by disease. Typhus. Have you ever seen the effect of that? It was a far cry from the golden court of the City of the Horizon.' For a moment he paused, the bitter lines around his mouth deepening. Then he continued.

'When the Khabiri attacked we were powerless against them. They are desert raiders. They slaughtered the men and the children, and took away the women. As I was an officer, they devised a special treat for me: they raped my wife and my ten-year-old daughter in front of me, three of them to each, sticking their penises into each of the gateways. Then they used their spears on them. They threw me from the battlements into the sea, but the rocks were merciless and did not kill me, though I have never longed for death so much as I did then. But a man must wait until Osiris calls him.' Merymose fell silent again.

'My *Ka* decided that I must live. I swam down the coast, carried by the current. When I got ashore I stole a small fishing boat and sailed it to the Delta. I joined the Medjays in the south, and served at Napata, before they posted me here.'

Huy cast around for something to say, and found nothing. When he did, it was awkward and inappropriate: 'You must hate us.'

'I hate no one. You cannot hate when you have died inside.'

After Merymose had gone, Huy closed up the house and walked down to the City of Dreams.

'Do you never sleep?' he said to Nubenehem, who was rooted to her couch in her half-reclining posture. There was a jar of thick yellow palm wine on the table beside her.

'Never when there is a living to be made,' she grinned. 'What do you want?'

'You mentioned a girl you said was my type.'

'Little Nefi? You're out of luck. She hasn't been back.'

'Did you give her work?'

'She was keen, but had no experience. To be frank I was going to give her to you to break in.' Nubenehem offered Huy the jar but he waved it away.

'Tell me what she looked like.'

'I did. Young. Innocent. Puppy fat on her cheeks. Plump young body. Very willing to show it off, she was. I wouldn't have minded turning her over myself.'

'Did you?'

Nubenehem's look became less friendly. 'No. These days I stick to less exhausting pleasures.' She indicated the wine jar. 'Why?'

'No reason.'

'Like to watch some of that, would you, women together?'

Huy paused. 'I am going to describe a girl to you. As exactly as I can. You tell me if that's the girl I missed.'

Summoning up as many details as he could remember, and trying to breathe life into her, Huy described Iritnefert.

'That's her,' said Nubenehem. 'So you found her after all. What was she doing? Working the docks?'

He was about to leave when the bead curtain was drawn aside and Kafy stood there. She looked at him resentfully.

'Well, well. Don't I know you from somewhere?'

Huy returned her gaze. Her eyes remained hard, but he knew it was an act. Her body was inviting him. He knew that it was an invitation he would accept. He took a step towards her.

Nubenehem held out her hand. 'Pay first,' she said.

The corridor beyond the bead curtain was long and dingy, lit every three or four paces by an oil lamp in a niche. Innumerable nights of such light had made the walls smoky. Muted sounds, and, once, a cry of pain, came from behind the closed doors that led off it on either side.

'Here we are,' said Kafy, stopping at a door which was open. The room beyond was cosy, lit by three lamps and heavy with dark blue drapery. Kafy slipped her hand under his kilt and closed it round his penis, smiling, pulling him into the room by it. He would not have liked to guess her age, had never seen her in anything other than half-light, and knew nothing about her beyond the fact that she came from a village to the north which, she had told him, stood in the shadow of the pyramid of Saqqara.

'Where have you been?' She asked.

'Nowhere.'

'Have you tired of me?'

'No.' He stopped her, taking her hands in his.

'What is it?' Her eyes stopped acting.

'One question.'

She looked resigned. 'You never stop working, do you?'

'There was a man here a few days ago. I saw him talking to Nubenehem. Well dressed, and perhaps elderly. I thought I knew him.'

'I didn't see him.'

'I think he had come for some sort of show. He paid well.'

Kafy's eyes lit up for a moment, and then shut him out. 'You'd better ask Nubenehem.'

'I did. She wouldn't tell me.'

She smiled. 'I'd help you if I could.' But her eyes were not smiling.

He knew he would get no more out of her, just as he knew she was getting impatient. He reached for her, pulling away the tight linen shift to expose a taut brown body with generous, firm breasts. Merymose's story had made him want to lose himself. He could not have stayed in his empty house.

She unknotted his kilt and sank to her knees, knowing how he liked to begin. 'It's been a long time; too long,' she smiled, slipping him into her mouth. As she bent forward, he saw that her left shoulder was disfigured by a terrible bruise.

* * *

60

A malevolent demon was standing on his head. It had buried its adze in his fontanelle, and was working the thing backwards and forwards methodically to split open his skull. Meanwhile two stonemasons inside his brain were using claw chisels to cut their way out through his eyes. He tried to sit up, but the most cautious movement threw his tormentors into a mania of activity and his stomach hurled a messy bile into his mouth. There was another taste. Figs.

Huy forced himself into a sitting position by degrees and brought the empty jar of fig liquor into vision. The raging optimism which it had instilled in him last night, under whose influence he had finally escaped from Merymose's story, was now replaced by a simple whimpering plea to whatever god listened to self-pitying hangover sufferers just to let him be all right again, his own man, as soon as possible. The only thing he was thankful for was that it was the eleventh day, the rest day. His binge would not have cost him his work.

Having at last managed to hold himself upright for five minutes without feeling the need to vomit, he started to order his heart. At first all that would come into it were moralising precepts about drink which he remembered from having to copy them as exercises when he was a student: I am told you go from street to street where everything stinks to the gods of alcohol. Alcohol will turn men away from you and send your soul to hell; you will be like a ship with a broken rudder, like a temple without its god, like a house without bread ... Whoever wrote that had never had unpleasant memories to drown, thought Huy, or been confronted with truths too horrible to face. On the other hand, when you resurfaced, there were the memories and the truths still; they had not gone away, and the only difference was that one was now less equipped to deal with them than before. That was what made men go on drinking, Huy supposed. A constant retreat; putting your senses to sleep rather than facing and destroying the cause of your distress. He wondered if Merymose ever drank heavily. Huy doubted it.

His head sang with pain and his stomach heeled over as he stood up, his hand flailing for the back of a chair to support him. Having got this far, he allowed himself another minute or so before confronting the thousand-day journey which separated him from the bathroom. Then, forcing himself to breathe regularly, he set off.

Later, having bathed and, if not eaten, at least drunk some herb tea, he felt that he might, after all, survive. He chewed coriander seeds to sweeten his breath and, feeling ready to face the world, had decided to put on his newest, cleanest kilt, with the leather sandals and the one headdress left from more prosperous days. He would try to gain access to the palace, if not to the houses of Ipuky and Reni. He did not hold out much hope that Merymose would persuade Kenamun to engage him, but there was no harm in familiarising himself with the terrain in advance if he could.

He was interrupted in dressing by a knock at the door, and opened it to a man he recognised, one of Taheb's body servants, an Assyrian who despite years in the Black Land still wore a long oiled black beard in ringlets. He touched his right hand to his forehead, lips and chest, and without a word presented a note to Huy, from Taheb, asking him to come to her immediately.

'Do you know what this is about?' he asked the Assyrian.

'No. But it is urgent. She is waiting for you, and look, she has sent her litter for you.'

By the time Huy arrived at the house he was free of the last traces of the tormentors in his head. He climbed down from the litter and the Assyrian conducted him not to the little courtyard but through the house to an upper room, whose high windows faced north to catch the wind. The room, painted a white so fresh that it seemed pale blue, was cool and soothing. Huy noticed a jug with wine and beakers set on a table made of white, polished wood and inlaid with river-horse ivory and gold. Beyond it, the west wall opened on to a wide balcony shaded by deep eaves supported on slender lotus-columns, which gave a view down across the city to the broad grey sweep of the river, sluggish and low at this time of year, but sacrificing none of its dignity. From here he could see the crowded harbour quarter, the rooftops so close together that they welded in the heat haze into one whole. Beyond them and further south sprawled the larger roofs of the palace compound, the buildings there, as he knew, separated by broad, shady boulevards paved with polished limestone kept regularly watered in case it should become too hot for the feet of the rich.

She did not keep him long. Dressed soberly in a long-sleeved, ankle-length tunic which, though cut loosely, came high up to her neck, she approached him with both hands extended in greeting.

'I am glad you are here. Have I taken you away from anything?'

'The Assyrian said you needed to see me urgently.'

'I thought I had better say that, or you might not come. You smell of corianders. That means you were drinking last night.'

'Yes. Merymose came to see me. He told me of his past.'

Taheb looked thoughtful. 'It is a sad story. But was that the only reason?'

'Something else, too.'

'Will you tell me?'

'No. Not now. Forgive me. It is nothing important. Nothing to do with Aset, either.'

She smiled a little sadly. 'Then I will not be curious, though it runs against my nature.'

'He wants my help. He has acquired a new chief. A priest called Kenamun.'

'Ah yes. The martinet.'

'He has never courted popularity.'

Taheb looked at him in surprise. 'Oh, but he has – with women.'

'And has he succeeded?'

'No.'

'What do you think of him?'

Taheb looked inwards before replying. 'He is a difficult man to impress. Not that I have ever tried.'

'I may have to.'

'Merymose is a braver man than I thought, if he is going to Kenamun of all people for the help of a former scribe of the Great Criminal!'

Taheb poured wine, which Huy was bound by etiquette to accept, though his heart resisted it. But to his surprise the drink was light, young, and faintly flavoured with honey, together with another taste, so subtle that he could not identify it. When he drank, the liquid flooded through him like sunlight.

'To life,' she said, toasting him.

'To life,' he replied.

She looked at him enigmatically for a moment, and then said, 'I have kept you from something. You look furtive.'

He smiled. 'I was planning to get into the palace.'

'Then you should have come to me first. They would never let you in alone, even though you are wearing your best clothes. Who were you hoping to pass yourself off as?' The same words might have been spoken through tight lips by the old Taheb. Now they came out spiced with delicate, ironic humour. Huy found it impossible not to relax.

'I should have thought,' he said. He was as sure as he could be of anything that Taheb was an ally to cultivate. Perhaps it was the effect of the enchanted drink, but he suddenly knew that what had made him hesitate before, her social rank, now seemed a ridiculous objection.

'I know Ipuky through Amotju, and Reni and my father were business associates.'

'Reni? You know about his daughter, then?'

'Yes. It is a tragedy. She was so trusting. Who can be doing this? Why?'

'There does not have to be a reason.' But Huy looked inwards.

Taheb smiled at him. 'You might as well ask me your questions, Huy. You are wondering how much I know, and *how* I know. It is because the rich in this city are in a club – news travels fast between families. It is hard to keep anything private but in this case privacy wasn't desired. People are frantic. Those with half-grown children are beginning to panic, especially those with girls.'

'Where are your children?'

'I have sent them to my brother in the Northern Capital until you solve this for us.'

'You have great faith.'

'If it is not the work of bad gods, you will solve it.'

'Chance is my only ally.'

'It is not such a terrible one.'

Their words hung in the air between them. Now they were silent. The atmosphere in the room became palpable, as if it had changed to clear, viscous fluid. It was not unpleasant, and Huy wondered whether it was the effect of the wine. Every pore of his skin felt aware, as sensitive as it did after the luxury of a hot bath. He was standing by the balcony. Taheb put down her wine, stood up, and crossed towards him. She took his beaker away and placed it on the balcony wall. Now her arms rested loosely on his bare shoulders, skin against skin. It burned.

'It's funny,' she murmured. 'Amotju was so slim and tall, and you are built more like a warrior or a boatman than a scribe.'

'My nickname at writing school was Bes. What did you put in the wine?'

'Just a little mandrake fruit. You haven't been in touch with me for an age, and I have wanted you since I saw you again at dinner. I wanted to be sure of you, you see.'

'Did you take some?'

'Of course. It heightens the fun. So they tell me. I have never tried it before.'

'Then how did you know the right dose?'

She laughed. 'Do you never stop asking questions? I want to feel you against me.'

Briefly her hands left him, darting behind her neck to undo a clasp. When she brought them away again, the dress fell like a curtain, revealing a strong body, broad shouldered but with slender hips and delicate breasts.

'Do you like what you see?'

Around him, the air swam gently, and he swam in it, with her, as his kilt, his sandals, his headdress, seemed to fall away. A couch had appeared on the balcony – had it always been there? – and they were lying on it together, though he could not remember moving to it.

She leant against him, their nipples touching, caressing his thighs with hers. Perhaps by magic, her hands were flowing with lotus oil, and with it her firm fingers anointed him.

Supporting her with his right arm, his left hand strayed from her breasts to her thigh, and from there slowly completed the journey to the mouth of the Cave of Sweet Mysteries, lingering long enough to find the little temple of Min and arouse him as she began to gasp for breath, her tongue making passionate sallies into his ear. He turned his face so that their lips could join, making another temple where their tongues embraced, stroking each other, running over teeth. Opening his eyes, he noticed a bloom of perspiration on her bronze shoulder, and slid his mouth over her skin to lick it off. Then he let his head fall to her breasts, taking each as far into his mouth as he could and teasing the nipples with his tongue. He lowered his head further, until he was drinking in the sweetness of her loins with his nose and his lips, kissing and teasing, sucking the tiny proud god who reared at the entrance to the Cave as she sighed and groaned softly far above him. Then she drew him up to her, and lowered her own head to take him in her mouth, her tongue darting out in tender forays at the base of his penis, stroking his belly with her hair as her teeth gently nibbled his manhood. Later she rose too, and their lips and tongues met again, full of sweet tastes.

Their hands were busy with each other, lubricated by the lotus oil, their perspiration and the wine of Min which had entered the mouth of the Cave. She held him firmly, pumping his penis up and down slowly and rhythmically, twisting it slightly as she did so. He bit his lip to curb the god, then buried his mouth in the curve where her neck met her shoulder, smelling her smell, wanting to drown in her.

They floated to the floor. Huy clasped her buttocks, his palms pressing hard against their softness, his fingertips urgently exploring that other cave they protected. With one hand Taheb did the same, while the other guided him into her. They cleaved to each other, lips hard against lips, bodies crushed together,

66

her heels against the small of his back, clinging there as they bucked and dived, soared and plummeted together. For two hours they made love, never leaving each other, even for the brief periods when they lay still, nibbling ears and lips gently; always delaying the splendour until the last possible moment, and always achieving it together, gasping and roaring, moaning and crying, seven times. At last they stopped, lying together, smelling the rich smell, feeling their sweat grow chill on them. Servants came, and wrapped them in soft new sheets together, and carried them to the bed which they had set up in the white room. Then they slept, hour upon hour, folded tightly together.

When he woke, it was to the sensation of her breath cool on his chest. When she woke, her eyes were like fires in the depths of the deepest wells. It was a long time before they spoke. Words had found their place.

They were of secondary importance.

FIVE

Kenamun was a tall man – too tall, with that fragile thinness which accompanies extreme height. His hands were large, with swollen knuckles and the long, nervous, hammer-ended fingers that betray a weak centre of life. They hung at the end of slender wrists and looked as if they had been tacked on to the wrong person. His head was long and bony, and so shaped that you could see all the contours of the skull beneath the skin. Here, too, the features were large, and clumsily applied: a nose like a ridge of clay, lips that recalled a Nubian's, though set in a bitter line; a protruding blue chin and ears so prominent that they covered half the sides of his head. Only his eyes were small, and they were set so deeply in their orbits that you could not tell what colour they were. They glittered like the backs of scarabs caught in torchlight at the rear of a tomb.

To mitigate his appearance, he had grown a beard – though it was so fine, to conform with custom, that it might have been painted on with a *kohl*-brush, an impression reinforced by the methodical severity with which the rest of the face had been shaved. He wore a red-and-gold headdress, and a white tunic trimmed with the same colours. He stood at an unusually high desk in the room into which Merymose ushered Huy, and there was no sign of any other furniture, beyond an open chest containing scrolls. Huy concluded that the man worked standing up.

He looked at Huy – as far as Huy could tell: it was more an impression of being looked at, and there was no reading the expression in the eyes – but spoke to Merymose without preamble.

'So this is the man you say is indispensable to us.'

'He would be of help,' said Merymose. 'We want this solved soon.'

'Indeed. But what methods has he that we do not have at our disposal already?'

'An instinct for asking the right questions.'

'Of whom? You know the families we are dealing with.'

'Frequently, just of himself.'

Kenamun had not removed his gaze from Huy, who began to feel like a specimen, or, worse, a snake stared down by a mongoose.

'You have recanted your allegiance to the Great Criminal?'

Huy sighed. 'I was not offered that possibility. I was merely forbidden to practise my profession.'

'And you were a scribe. After all those years of training, that must have been like having your hand cut off.' Kenamun considered. 'But you were not sent into exile, or to work in the mines?'

'No.'

'And you are a friend of the family of Amotju?'

'Yes,' said Huy, recalling Taheb. Could that have only been yesterday – and at about this time?

The official dropped his gaze abruptly and turned his attention to some papers on his desk. 'You are a good officer, Merymose,' he said at last, 'and although I disagree with you about the capability of our Medjays, I respect your judgment. You may consult this man, but he is to have no direct or unsupervised contact with the families of the girls, and he is to work only under your orders, not independently. You will make a report to me daily at the first hour of night. Finally, he is your responsibility. If this becomes widely known, I will say that you acted on your own initiative, and you will take the consequences.'

He did not look up, or say anything more. Huy and Merymose glanced at each other, and withdrew.

'What is he like?' asked Huy as soon as they were clear of the building and out in the broad street that ran close to the walls of the palace complex. After Kenamun's office, the light of day seemed even brighter, the sun warmer.

'He is an official. He is on his dignity. He doesn't know how to go about the work he has been put in charge of, and yet the successful solution of this case will be a great coup for him, politically. On the other hand, the risk is high, because failure will set him back. He has few friends, and already the pressure Ipuky and Reni are putting on him through their friends is filtering down to me. But he made no objection to engaging you. That is a degree of how desperate he is to get this thing settled.'

They walked down to the river, as a motley crowd milled about the jetties where the ferry boats left for the West Bank. Over there, generations of pharaohs slept in the tombs, cut deep into the red cliffs of the valley. The thought of the neglected tomb of Nefertiti passed briefly through Huy's mind.

'What do the families say?'

'They are too broken in spirit to know. There is suspicion of the work of demons; but it is rare for demons to attack the rich, and above all to leave no trace of violence on the bodies. That there is a clear similarity has escaped no one, and there is fear that other daughters of similar families are at risk. We have been pestered for men to protect several houses, and as these people have such influence, we cannot refuse.'

'The girls must have had friends. Have you spoken to them?' Huy decided to keep what he had learnt about Iritnefert to himself for the moment. There was no point in telling Merymose what could not be proved. There was little likelihood that he would believe it, and, anyway Huy himself was not about to trust the Medjay completely.

'Yes, some. Of course the two girls knew each other, too – all part of the same set. It seems that Ipuky's daughter was rebellious; but they either don't know what she got up to, or won't say. The other girl – ' Merymose hesitated.

'Yes?'

'Nothing. Just an ordinary girl.'

Huy nodded, but the hesitation had not escaped him.

'Her brothers are angry,' continued Merymose more confidently.

'At least, one is angry; the other is inclined to be more . . .'

he searched for the word, 'philosophical about it – like his father.'

'Philosophical?' Huy imagined the rage he would feel if his son were killed.

'They accept what has happened; but they do not see anger as the fuel for vengeance. I know that Ipuky is putting his own men on to this.'

'That will muddy the water.'

'What do you want them to do? Medjays are not trained to investigate such things as these,' repeated Merymose.

'And if it is a demon?'

'The household priests are looking to Osiris for guidance. So far he has given none. The household priests take that to mean that the gods are not responsible for these deaths.'

Huy wondered how deep Merymose's belief in the gods ran. Also, being human, Huy regretted that he was now committed to working with the policeman. If he had been able to, how gladly he would have hired himself out to either of the wealthy men whose daughters had died. He doubted if the authorities represented by Merymose and Kenamun would pay him as much as Reni or Ipuky would have; and he doubted if he would receive any reward at all if he were unsuccessful.

He looked up to see Merymose grinning at him. 'I know what you are thinking,' he said. 'Neither of them would have engaged you. Now that we have an escaped political prisoner on the loose, everybody is fighting shy of having anything to do with people like you. Of course it doesn't affect the really big fish, but even important officials who recanted formally are looking over their shoulders at the moment. That these killings have happened at the same time doesn't help.'

'Then thank you for getting me any work at all.' Huy countered affability with affability; but he could not help wondering what strings Merymose had had to pull – or how – to get Kenamun to accept him. He wondered if he should not give his *Ka* a name, and call it Taheb.

'What did you tell them at the paperworks?'

'They didn't ask questions. I'd given them time to look for

someone to replace me permanently. And they told me that I can have a job back there any time I want.' Huy grinned. Nothing would drag him back to that grind.

They had reached the end of the ferry jetties and ahead of them lay the tightly-knit bulk of the town, its few colours – beige, dun, ochre, brown and white – flattened by the sunlight. The shadows provided some relief, and here and there a man or a donkey dozed in one. A thin dog sidled up to them, stopping just out of range of a kick, and looked at them with what it hoped was an appealing expression. It only succeeded in looking craven.

'We've nothing for you,' Merymose told the dog, adding to Huy: 'If you're poor *and* ugly, you can forget about love, eh?'

'What do you want to do?' asked Huy.

'I want to tell you everything I know about all this so far, and in detail. What do you want to do?'

'I want to look at the bodies.'

Merymose hesitated again. 'We'll have to get permission from the families. They will both be with the embalmers.'

'Then let's do that. Fast.'

'But what can you possibly tell from the bodies, especially now?'

'They must have died somehow. It may be that looking at the bodies will tell me. I might see something that has been missed.'

'They may have been poisoned.'

'Poison takes time, and it hurts, it turns the lips black. Iritnefert looked peaceful, and her body was relaxed. From what you say, Reni's daughter did not look different. What was her name? You never mentioned it.'

'Neferukhebit. They called her Nefi.'

Huy's stomach leapt, but he hid his surprise from Merymose. The policeman was keeping things from him. Why? Was it just that he was obeying orders from above?

'What did she look like?'

Merymose told him. Huy hoped that the embalmers knew their job, and had preserved the bodies well. He told himself that he had little to fear; but he was sweating as they made their way into the city.

Meet by the water, he had told her. Lying waiting for the family to go to sleep, she had begun to lose courage. Perhaps, she had thought, she would not go after all. She would stay, safely in bed, cocooned in the fresh linen sheets scented with *seshen*, and then perhaps later she would explain, if the opportunity arose. It might not even be necessary.

But then her pride and her curiosity had got the better of her again, and she remembered why she had agreed to the meeting in the first place. The thought of what might happen scared her, but it thrilled her too. Of course, nothing at all might happen. They might just talk. But that would be a kind of failure, having summoned up the courage to go this far, to take this step; and though he had warned her that it might hurt a little, she trusted him: he was so gentle, so mature. He would not do her any real harm.

Once she was certain that the house was asleep she had climbed lightly out of bed, dipping her face into the bowl of washing water on the table near the door and dabbing it dry with a hand towel. She was careful not to disturb the make-up she had applied secretly before retiring, and checked it quickly in a polished bronze mirror that lay next to the bowl, the deep yellow glow from the oil lamp she had left burning providing her with just enough light to see that none had smudged. Having satisfied herself, she slipped into a tight calf-length dress which had a strap over the left shoulder but which fell away to the right of her body, leaving one young breast exposed. Then she snuffed out the light, and waited for a moment, getting her owl-vision. High in the sky, Khons's chariot reflected only a sliver of light from its sides.

Stepping into the passage she trod on something soft, silky and alive, but was in time to withdraw her naked foot before it wailed. Instead, a sleepy purring trill told her that the dozing house cat – it was the long-haired one, named after Bubastis, and almost a pet – had mistaken her clumsiness for a caress; she had barely disturbed its sleep. The corridor was in the

73

embrace of a deep silence which spread right across the dark garden court below and beyond the open verandah which ran along all four inward-looking walls of the house on the first floor, on to which the bedrooms opened. The only sound was her father's heavy breathing, occasionally broken by a snore. She stole past his door with even greater care, unsure whether he was sleeping alone tonight. It had been long since he had asked her mother to share his bed, and for some time now his favourite had been a young Khabiri concubine, a month younger than she was herself. And that, if anything, was what had fired her to embark on this adventure.

Aware of the loose board near the top of the stairs, she clung to the wall and then slipped down to the garden in shadow, barely a shadow herself, and making as little noise, though inside her head it seemed as if her heart would waken the dead with its pumping. The one hurdle still to be jumped was the gatekeeper; but she had chosen her night carefully. Old Mahu was on duty, and he never left his shelter by the main gate, once he was sure that everyone was asleep. It was likely that he, too, slept.

She made her way to the small side gate that opened on to the alley and which in the daytime was kept permanently open so that tradesmen could make their way to the kitchens through the vegetable garden. There was a steady flow of people during the day and in theory the last to use the gate after the second hour of night should be the one responsible for bolting it. In practice this rarely happened, and anyway since childhood, even before she was old enough to wear her hair in the Lock of Youth twisted over her right shoulder, she had known the location of the hidden bolt, and how to slide it.

She was not wearing her hair tied into the Lock now. It was loose and tumbled in a dark brown cascade over her narrow shoulders. It changed her face; she seemed a stranger, a complete adult. She tried to imagine how she would look when she was old enough to wear a wig, like her mother and the great ladies of the court who surrounded Queen Ankhsenpaamun, though the queen was not much older than she was herself.

For once the little gate was locked, but she quickly pulled

back the stone bolt and slipped outside, drawing the gate closed but not relocking it: she would need to be as little delayed as possible if she were to get back unnoticed, and the first servants rose early, at the ninth hour of night. She knew by the temperature that it was now about the sixth hour. Borne on a tiny breeze, there was even a faint hint of morning in the air already, so she would have to hurry.

She knew the meeting place; the pool in the little park on the south side of the palace compound. She knew it because she frequently went there. The pool in their own garden had been filled in by her father five years before when her baby brother had drowned there; but she loved to sit by cool water, inured to the stinging flies which gave people from the north so much trouble. And now she was going there again, for a great adventure; perhaps the greatest in her life. The anticipation overcame her fear, and there was fear: the thing which had most made her hesitate was the thought of the deaths of her two friends. But Iritnefert had been found by the river, outside the compound; and Neferukhebit in her own home. Besides, she would not be alone – only on the journey there and back. During the hour they would be together, she would be protected. The thought gave wings to her feet. She did not want to waste a moment of the time they would have.

She arrived at the park. It was cool and dark, but familiar, and she felt no fear as she entered it, though she briefly touched the *tjet* amulet at her neck for luck. She was aware of her body, realising that it was taut as a lute string with anticipation. Every pore was alive. She could feel the root of every hair of her head.

She advanced through the shadows less cautiously, her only fear now that there would be no one to meet her. The thought cast darkness over her heart.

But there, standing at the edge of the pool, half-hidden in the deeper shade cast by a clump of leaning palm trees, he was waiting. Reassuring, smiling at her, and coming to greet her. Strange that he should seem so familiar to her now; as if they had always been close.

'You came.'

She looked up at him, wanting to reach up and stroke his face. His eyes held her. She had no will.

'I never doubted that you would.'

'I am on fire,' she said, and was immediately ashamed of her candour.

He moved away from her. Only a fraction, but she was aware of it.

'This is a solemn moment. We must consecrate it to each other and to the gods.'

'Yes.' She was too awed to notice anything but passion in the voice. She knew from pictures in the *Book of Instruction* clandestinely glimpsed in her father's library what to expect, approximately; and she had seen animals; but exactly what happened she could not imagine.

'We do not want the gods to regard our deed as evil.'

'They wouldn't do that. It is good to create life.'

'But in an evil world innocence must be protected. Come. The water will purify us.'

She watched as if dreaming as he untied his kilt, all he was wearing, and let it fall to the warm ground beneath them. She looked between his legs, but all was shadow there until he turned towards her and she saw the snake's head loom. Her first sensation was of unfocused disappointment. It was not as large or as upright as the one in the *Book of Instruction*.

'Now you.'

Dutifully, even hastily, she pulled the strap down over her left arm and stepped out of her dress. She regretted that it was too dark for him to see how beautiful she had tried to make herself, even using malachite as well as the usual galena. She let the dress fall and took a shy step towards him. He put out a hand and caressed her hair, her head, with tenderness and, she thought, curious detachment. But she knew nothing of these things.

Then he was closer. There was the warm, acrid male smell of his body, and his left arm was round her, stronger than she thought, holding her against him. Her face was against his chest. Clumsily, for he was holding her too tightly for her to manoeuvre, she kissed him there, but he twisted away, bruising her lips and leaving her confused and rejected. What had she done wrong?

'Teach me,' she said, raising her head to look at him.

He did not look into her eyes. He was steadying her with his left arm, fumbling with something in his right hand. She was held so tightly now that she could not struggle. Then at last his lips descended on hers and she closed her eyes.

The pain which followed immediately was so sudden and so extreme that it went beyond feeling. She opened her eyes but he kept his arm tightly round her, his lips pressed on hers, so she could not move. But the will do to so did not last. What seemed an age was only seconds, fractions of seconds, before her open eyes no longer responded to the light they received. The side of his face became a range of grey hills towards which she was riding, on some animal whose hoofs did not touch the ground. Then the hills merged into the dark sky behind them, and all was grey, but it was not the hoped-for grey which is the beginning of dawn. It was a grey that went deeper, and deeper, into night.

SIX

They took the brain from her head with long hooks, delicately drawing the tissue out through her nostrils, and discarding it in a small brazier of red-hot charcoal. The brain was of no importance. Then they used water mixed with vinegar in a syringe to rinse the cavity clear, sitting her up so that the residue could run out through her nose. Afterwards, they carefully cleaned her face before the flies could settle.

The vital organs, the stomach, the intestines, the lungs and the liver, were withdrawn carefully and whole. The embalmers laid her flat on a long wooden table, and one of them, the master, took a sharp flint knife to make a long incision low down in her side. Probing with his narrow hands he located the organs he sought, and, using another slender knife, dislodged and withdrew them, handing them to his assistant, who placed them in bronze trays and took them to another table where he covered them with natron salt, to dry and preserve them ready for the four jars which would stand in a chest at the head of the coffin. Their eternal resting place.

Once he had cleared the body, the master embalmer rinsed it through, first with palm wine, and then with a solution of coriander. He would now dry it in natron, before packing the cavities he had made with linen treated with myrrh and cassia; the nostrils and eyes plugged with linen soaked in resin, and the hair dressed with as much care as for attendance at a royal wedding.

The master embalmer had seven bodies laid out in various stages of the seventy-day preparation for eternity, and the open-ended hall where he worked was crowded. He had employed two extra assistants to keep the flies at bay, and he found he had to force himself not to hurry his craft, not to cut corners. His clients were rich and demanding, and all the more likely to notice a botched job. His hall was built on a north-to-south axis, so that the wind blew through it constantly, keeping the air fresh; but the odours of the spices and scented oils he used were the only ones a visitor might smell. All moisture was drawn out of the dead before they could rot.

It had taken a full day for Merymose to obtain permission for Huy to visit the embalmer. By the time he'd got it, the two dead girls the scribe wanted to see had been joined by this third. Her body had been found the morning before by the side of the pool in the little park on the south side of the royal compound. Now, Huy was visiting the embalmer alone, barely repressing his fury at the delay, but for which a girl's life might have been saved. Inwardly, too, he cursed the arrogance of the latest victim's father. Above all he turned his anger towards Kenamun, who, on grounds of security, had forbidden Huy to visit the scene of the third murder when it came to light, where he might have had a chance at last of studying the circumstances of death.

Merymose had already seen the body, but now he had been deputed by an increasingly impatient Kenamun to visit the victim's parents. The father was a general, a commander of cavalry, and the mother a daughter of the army's chief supplier of salt. The father had not applied for a Medjay to guard his house, giving as his reason that he had efficient men of his own to do the job.

'She was called Mertseger,' the embalmer told Huy as he stood looking down at her. 'She looks terrible now, but I'm going to put packing in the cheeks to fill them up again after I've dried her out. The loss of moisture makes the face cave in, look like a skull. But I'll give her back her beauty.'

The cavity of her abdomen had dropped alarmingly with the removal of its contents. The dark incision running obliquely from just above her vagina seemed a grosser violation of her corpse than anything inflicted on her in life.

'Did you notice anything, any wound?'

'No. And she had never known a man. The skin is unbroken,' he gestured professionally towards the vagina. 'I don't need a doctor to tell me that. Do you want to see?'

'No.'

'I'll stitch it up when she has dried out. We seal all the openings to the body. It is an extra insurance against the maggots. Once the flies have laid their eggs on a body, there's nothing we can do, so we get that seen to as quickly as possible.'

Huy turned to the two adjoining tables. On the one farthest away lay Iritnefert, her arms at her sides, held there stiffly, as if she wanted to deny the downward pull of the earth. Her head was back and her chin raised, resin plugging the eye sockets. An assistant was carefully applying gold leaf to it. The lack of eyes robbed the face of all the character it had had, of personality, of the vestige of life. Huy hoped that when he died it would be in the desert or on the river, so that the vultures or the crocodiles would take him. He did not like the idea of being closed in a black tomb, though he knew that it would be only his *Sahu* lying there.

Nevertheless he looked more closely at Iritnefert.

Nothing to tell now of the girl she had been. The nose, dried out, was pitifully thin and pinched. The cheeks, also awaiting padding, had vanished into the cavities of the skull. She looked like a leathery caricature of the old woman she might have become.

'She'll look as alive as you or me, once we've packed her and made up her face,' the embalmer reassured him again. 'Normally we don't like people to see them at this stage. It's better that way. It's better for them to see their loved ones as they remember them.'

Huy looked at the man. They were about the same age, but the embalmer seemed older. His hands were soft and wax-like from frequent washing. He was of medium height, and had regular, even features of the kind which are instantly forgettable. His dark face was framed by raven-black hair so perfectly cut that it barely changed its set as he moved. His expression was one of amused and slightly sinister detachment, which reminded Huy strangely of the young king's. You could imagine Tutankhamun sparing a man on the point of execution, or ordering the death of thousands, without the slightest twitch of an eye muscle.

'I want to see the second one – Neferukhebit,' said Huy briskly. He had had enough of carrying on at a snail's pace. If toes had to be trodden on, too bad. Merymose might get it in the neck from Kenamun, but if this madman was to be nailed quickly, the odd official would have to sacrifice his dignity.

The embalmer sniffed primly. 'That is impossible. As you can see.'

High walls of planking surrounded the body on the second table, forming a trough at the bottom of which the body lay. Into this natron salt had been poured, covering the corpse completely.

'How long does this take?' Huy insisted impatiently.

'It depends on the weather, on the time of year, on the size of the body. In this case, not more than thirty days – forty at the most.'

'And how long has it been so far?'

The embalmer consulted the writing on a limestone flake attached to the edge of the trough. He tutted, sucked his teeth.

'How much difference would it make if you cleared this away for a few minutes – that's all?' persisted Huy. 'It is important that I see her.'

'I've told you; it's impossible. Nobody has ever suggested anything of the sort ever before. It is unheard of.' The embalmer was shocked.

Huy forced himself to stay patient. 'I imagine it is impossible for just anyone to come in here to see your work, as I have?'

'Quite impossible.'

'And you know that I am only here because I have royal authority?'

'Yes.'

'That authority is given me to help me find the killer of these girls.'

The embalmer looked uncomfortable, and wiped the back

of his neck with a cloth. His assistants looked across with studiously blank faces as Huy began to raise his voice. The embalmer himself eyed him more nervously. This stocky little man, whose educated voice belied his riverman appearance, looked capable of doing damage. The embalmer glanced to check how close he was to a narrow shelf on which a series of knives were arranged in orderly rows.

'It is not just me you will be obstructing when you object to my seeing her body.'

'But to interrupt the process – '

'For a few minutes?'

'It has never been done before. I don't know what the effect will be. I'd need the parents' permission.'

Huy had had enough. 'You have it,' he lied firmly.

'In writing?'

Huy growled, taking a step forward. 'You doubt my word? I'm an officer of the court.'

Still doubtful, the embalmer beckoned his assistants away from their other tasks. He was probably thinking that in these times it was not worth taking the risk of offending anyone, just in case they were agents of Horemheb and you ended up in an emerald mine on the Eastern Coast. Together, the three of them removed the boards which formed the trough and the natron ran off in a tide of white powder on to the floor. Huy noticed the dessicated corpse of a shrew which must have fallen in when the stuff was first poured over Neferukhebit.

She emerged like a piece of sculpture from the white tide – the first woman, born of rock. Fussily, the embalmer dusted the remains of the salt from her body. The last of it to come away was damp, and a faint odour of sweet mustiness clung to it. Huy was surprised that it was not more unpleasant.

'Quickly,' said the embalmer.

Huy looked at her, reaching over to brush a last detail of natron away from her face.

Already the features were changing as moisture was drawn out of the flesh, but remembering how Iritnefert had looked when he had first seen her, he could understand how the two girls could be confused. They might have been twins. And, he reflected, the same innocence, the same near-perfect regularity of feature, was shared by Mertseger, who lay two paces away in the patience of death, awaiting her preparation for the Fields of Aarru.

'I need to look at her back,' he said after several minutes of carefully examining the girl's body.

'That *is* impossible.'

Huy dismissed the embalmer with a look and abruptly motioned to the two assistants. 'Come on. She can't be heavy.'

The assistants looked from Huy to their chief, who nodded assent. It was a more difficult job than they had imagined, because of the stiffness of the limbs, but by holding the head and the ankles they managed it. Huy looked carefully at the girl's back, and found what he was seeking. If only Nubenehem remembered it, then at least he could establish for certain which girl had been at the City of Dreams. If whoever had killed her had also seen her there, and could be identified . . . Well, it would be progress, of a sort.

He nodded his thanks and the men laid her back on the table. The embalmer helped them replace the planks, and then fussed about whether to sweep up and re-use the original natron, or replace it with fresh salt. While he was deliberating, another thought suddenly struck Huy, and he leant over the edge of the trough, feeling the girl's stomach and breasts.

'What are you doing?' the embalmer asked, outraged.

Huy felt under the small breasts and raised them. Under the left, just visible, was a minute puncture. Quickly, he moved across to Iritnefert's body. The skin under the breasts had puckered and darkened, and it was impossible to see anything. He made his way back past Neferukhebit to where Mertseger lay. Under her left breast, whose pale skin was only just beginning to give up its bloom to death, was a tiny, dark-red blob, no bigger than a sand flea.

Armed with his new knowledge, Huy hastened back to the centre of the capital, but Merymose was not to be found. As it was possible that the Medjay had left word at his house, Huy went home. There was no message from the police captain, and he was on the point of leaving again for the City of Dreams when a rickshaw, its linen sunscreens pulled down around the passenger seat, rushed into the square and stopped by him, blocking his path.

Surere was already looking sleeker, Huy thought, as he tried to banish the servile feelings which still rose to the surface when he found himself in the company of his former superior. Surere, presumably, had sent for him because he needed his help; why was it, then, that he gave the impression of bestowing a favour?

'It was a risk, sending a letter to my house,' said Huy.

Surere spread his hands. 'It would have been a greater one to have visited you in person. And the boy who served as my messenger is illiterate – a rare gift in a servant.'

Huy pursed his lips. He had never liked the nakedness with which Surere used people. Even less did he like the way in which people continued to be taken in by him. He remembered asking a fellow scribe about this, years ago, as they stood in one of the sun-filled courtyards of the Great Archive at Akhetaten.

'I can't stand his lordliness; but I admire his moral stance; and the first is always the servant of the second,' the other scribe had explained serenely, fuelling Huy's dislike. Still, Huy had answered Surere's summons, had even given in to the messenger's insistence that they travel in the closed rickshaw, so that he would not be able to tell where they were going. They had gone on for a long distance, before arriving at a door in a long, anonymous wall; the letter bearer, a gloomily serious young man with eyebrows which met across his brow, maintaining a severe silence throughout the journey. And now this room.

'You haven't said what you want.'

'That would have been foolish, in such a letter.' The bantering tone remained in Surere's voice but he added edge to it for the last word or two. Huy felt himself warned. By this man who had no power over him and whom he could sink with one word to Merymose. But treachery was not in

84

Huy's blood. He looked around the miserable room in which they were standing: a low, dark, cramped place with a grudging little window through which thin light crept apologetically. It fell on a rough table and two stools. On the table were a jug of water and two wooden beakers, together with a small bowl of salt and a cob of dark bread. The walls were unpainted, mud-brown, and bare of any decoration or shelf. No table stood by the plain low bed in the corner, the only other piece of furniture in the room.

'How long have you been here?' asked Huy.

'Thirty days.'

'And how long will you stay?'

'Until I am ready to leave. My preparations are well advanced; but there has been other business to attend to here.'

'What?' Huy tried to keep the sharpness out of his voice. He regretted the abruptness of the question, but Surere did not appear to have noticed.

'Simply the question of funds. Even here, I have found there are those who remain loyal to the New Thinking. I am surprised you do not know of them.'

Surere had managed to obtain a wig that rose high on the crown and fell heavily over the back and shoulders. It was raven black and the hair was entwined with a slim rope of gold thread and opals. He wore a light yellow tunic which reached the knee, and on his feet were leather sandals with decorated metal buckles. Whoever was looking after Surere was not short of money, however simply the man was lodged.

'You are admiring my finery,' smiled Surere.

'Your source of funds is a rich one.'

'There are men here who remember me, who owe me favours and do not forget.'

Huy wondered if the community which was supporting Surere was less one that adhered to the New Thinking in secret than one which simply shared his sexual habits. The Black Land had never condemned men or women who loved their own kind, or those who crossed the frontiers between loving those of the same and the opposite sex; but minorities formed fraternities, and members of the clubs would do each other good turns when they could. Harbouring an escaped *political* of Surere's importance, though, hardly came under the banner of simple mutual back-scratching.

'I am surprised that you do not have more enemies than friends here.'

Surere smiled. 'Does it amuse you to state the obvious? Luckily I have many loyal friends here – more, perhaps, than you do. And in places you would least suspect.'

'You are more fortunate than most of the survivors of the City of the Horizon,' said Huy. 'More fortunate than I am, or Paheri, for example.'

Surere's eyes gave away his thought before he could stop them. 'What do you know of Paheri?'

'Is he here? Ipuky is a powerful man – he could have extended his protection to his son.'

'Paheri is dead.'

'How do you know?'

'Do not talk of him. To speak his name invites evil.'

'That is not the belief of one who trusts the Aten.'

'Do not *talk* of him, Huy.' Surere's voice was serious, beseeching.

'And yet you live like this,' remarked Huy, indicating the room, forced to let the question of Paheri hang in the air. The former *nomarch*'s panic at the mention of his old deputy's name was a lead of sorts, but it was a fish that would have to be played.

Surere's gaze became hard. 'Yes. It is necessary. Don't forget that I am in hiding. I cannot start to live again as I used to.' He broke off, and when he spoke again, his tone had changed. It was as if two *Kas* battled for control of him.

'There is another reason,' he continued in a softer voice. 'I need to harden myself for my new destiny.'

'For the desert?' asked Huy cautiously.

'Yes.' Huy saw that Surere spoke with absolute seriousness. He thought again about how the changes which had occurred in the Southern Capital, to which Surere had now been exposed after so long away, might have affected such an inflexible heart.

'But your time in the quarries must have strengthened your muscles.'

'That is true. But my resolve must also be disciplined. Before my fall, when I was a great man, I was tempted by meat and wine, and by the luxuries my position brought me. But these things belong to the past. I have a new mission.' Surere leant forward and his head, for the first time, was fully illuminated by the narrow shaft of light that fell through the window. His face was set. There was not a trace of irony in his expression and in his eyes Huy discerned a coldness and distance he had not noticed before.

'What is it?' he asked, more cautiously.

'To bring our people back to the innocence they enjoyed under the old king.'

'That is dangerous talk. And was it ever *innocence*?'

'The tree was destroyed before it could bear fruit!' shouted Surere, gripping the edge of the table and half rising from his seat. He quickly controlled himself, however, and continued more calmly. 'That is why I asked you to meet me. You could help me. You could be my lieutenant.'

Huy said nothing, pausing a fraction too long, seeking some reply.

'You hesitate?' persisted Surere. 'I thought you were still one of us!'

'I do not know what I believe,' said Huy. 'The New Thinking touched the elite. It made no difference to the people. Now, the Northern Empire is lost, and the Black Land is in a chaos it has not known since Nebphetyre Amosis, two hundred years ago!'

'Do you think any of this would have happened if Akhenaten had not been thwarted? If it hadn't been for the machinations of Horemheb . . .'

Surere broke off in fury. Huy looked round instinctively. His former colleague had been speaking loudly, and his talk was treasonable. He did not have time now to investigate his own feelings, but somewhere at the back of his mind was the thought that he was, himself, no idealist. He had to live with things as they were, and his work, as far as it existed, was on the plane of helping individuals who had to live, as he did, in the society which existed. The idea of going into the deserts of the north to found a new religious colony had no attraction for him, and he was beginning to think that, for all the patina of civilisation which he had reassumed, Surere's years of imprisonment had cost him his reason. Who was protecting him? If they did not know all of his plans, they would be placing themselves in great danger. If they did know, then perhaps they intended to follow Surere into the desert.

'When do you intend to leave?'

'Soon.'

'When?'

Surere looked at him for a long time. 'Despite your apostasy,' he said finally, his mouth twisted bitterly, 'I do not think you will betray me. Perhaps it is simply that you do not have the courage to do so. But I will trust you, because there are few with whom I can talk as I can talk to you. And perhaps what I tell you will, even now, change your mind. Do not be a disappointment to me, Huy.'

His tone had changed again, and now he spoke like a worried father who still lives in hope for his son. Huy saw that to play along was the only way to get more information, and Surere had mentioned the protection of innocence as the mainstay of his creed often enough now for the scribe to make connections, though they were as yet half-formed, and his heart was inclined, at their birth, to reject them as falling too pat. Had not Paheri broken with his master for relaxing his severity, though?

'Tell me,' he asked, feigning submission.

Surere looked at him searchingly before, satisfied that he could place his trust here, and also in need of an audience, he began:

'Think of our Great Queen, Nefertiti.'

Huy recalled that magnificent woman. The gentle, careful, intelligent eyes that gave nothing away while leaving you with the impression that you and what you were saying were the most intelligent things she had ever beheld and heard. Even the fine portrait bust they had made of her did no justice to her living beauty.

'She was taken away too early in the Boat of the Night.' The queen had been twenty-two.

'Her life here was fulfilled,' said Huy, repeating the stock formula.

'You cannot say that! I knew her better than anyone but the king. I was devoted to her, and she rewarded my devotion with her trust.'

Huy pictured the neglected tomb in the Valley, and wondered if Surere was thinking of it too.

'She had seven daughters by the king,' continued Surere. 'Seven daughters and no sons. And yet he never sought another Great Wife. He knew the fruit of their loins was ordained by Aten. Seven vessels of purity, destined to bear great children, to carry the New Thinking throughout the world, even beyond the Great Green, and south beyond the forests to the sea again.'

Huy looked at him. Beyond the Great Green and the lands to the north of it, he knew, was the world's end. A rocky coast, a scattering of wild islands.

The forests to the south had never been crossed. The world's end lay there too.

'And what has happened to them?' Surere went on.

The last princess had been born too soon and too tiny to live. The oldest, whom the king her father had also married, later took as her husband his successor, Smenkhkare. The second daughter had died in childhood; the fifth and sixth princesses, still children, were virtual prisoners of Horemheb in the royal palace of the Southern Capital, together with their aunt Nezemmut, Nefertiti's younger sister; and though treated with all the deference their rank demanded, they were never allowed anywhere unattended by a corps of Horemheb's own men.

The fourth sister, the one who had found the child in a basket on the banks of the river, and insisted on adopting him, had married Burraburiash of Babylon and long since left the Black Land. Her adopted son Ra-Moses was now a junior officer in the Army of the Northern Frontier.

'One of them is married to our present king,' Huy said quietly. The third sister, Ankhsenpaaten, had been given as a child bride to Tutankhaten. When he became pharaoh, they changed their names in honour of the Old Religion – he to Tutankhamun, she to Ankhsenpaamun. The old god of the Southern Capital, Amun, with his wife Mut the Vulture and his son Khons the Moon Sailor, had returned in triumphant trinity.

'Yes!' said Surere bitterly. 'And see how she has rewarded the memory of her father. It would be better if she had died.'

'You cannot say that.'

'I can! I can say it with authority.'

'Whose?'

Surere's voice dropped. 'I will tell you. The king's.'

Huy looked at him closely, unsure how to react, even what to think. Surere was returning his gaze out of candid, friendly eyes; convinced eyes. The eyes of a madman.

'On the authority of which king?' asked Huy carefully, not wanting to break the fragile atmosphere.

'Akhenaten.' Surere's stare did not waver. It became more triumphant. 'You see? He has not abandoned us. Huy, abandon your cynicism. Do not go back to the old gods.'

Huy sat fixed to his stool, his heart still. It could be that the king had returned. But why now? And why to Surere?

'You are sure?' He knew how banal the question was as soon as he had asked it, but it did not affect Surere's mood.

'I am as sure of it as I am of this water.'

'What did he look like?'

Surere made a gesture of impatience. 'Like himself. Do you think I only saw his *Ba*? Do you think the king would have a mere *Ba*? A little feathered thing with a human head? No, it was himself, in his body, the Eight Elements reunited.'

'Where did you see him?'

Surere suddenly looked crafty. 'Too many questions, little brother. No; now it is for me to speak and you to listen.'

Huy spread his hands submissively, but then winced in pain as Surere suddenly leant forward and seized his shoulder, the strength of ten men in his large, bony hand.

'His daughter has disappointed him; that is why she has no children,' continued Surere. 'That was the first thing he told me. He is distressed by what the Black Land has become, so soon after his departure for the Fields of Aarru. That is why he cannot rest there. He hears the voice of his people constantly, calling him. And now he has returned to help them, through his chosen disciples.'

Surere stopped, to see what effect his words were having on Huy. Huy sat in silence, hoping that his expression betrayed nothing of his thoughts.

'My own instincts were correct, little brother,' continued Surere, repeating the term of endearment. 'I had strayed from the path of true justice, and used people for my own ends. I see now how wrong I was, and yet when I told the king that without resorting to such action I would still be in the granite quarries and so unable to do his bidding, he understood and forgave me. I even believe he sent Khaemhet the boatman to be my lover and my liberator.' He paused for a moment, looking past Huy's shoulder, far away, before continuing, but without releasing his tenacious grip.

'I was right about the Black Land. Without the moral strength of the New Thinking it will fall back into the old corruption. Imagine, Huy. For two thousand years we lived in darkness. The light dazzled us for a bare ten years with its brilliance, before it was extinguished. Our task is to rekindle it. Will you not help me?'

He paused again, this time clearly waiting for an answer. 'Gladly,' replied Huy cautiously. 'But my place is not in the desert. Surely, there is work to do here too.'

Surere made a dismissive gesture with one elegant arm. 'The capitals are doomed. This Southern Capital especially, the seat of – I can barely bring myself to utter the name – Amun, the False One, the Pretender. It is a city of futile dreams, my friend. And without the True Light, the Black Land is doomed.'

'And the king told you all this?' Huy felt cold. Outside, the sun still shone, though with the approach of evening the light had lost some of its force and the room grew dimmer. It was cold here. He watched a lizard scuttle furtively along the join between wall and ceiling, and disappear into a crevice.

To Huy's relief, his shoulder was released. It throbbed. He wanted to rub it, but the *balanos* for the bruise that would grow there would have to wait until later. 'I offered him my thoughts. I opened my heart to him, and he gave me his blessing.'

'Did he give you any . . . orders?'

For a moment, Surere was confused; then his expression cleared. 'He will, in his time.'

'And where will he give you them? In the desert?'

'If he chooses. He smiles on my plan.'

'You have collected followers, I suppose?'

Surere looked at him serenely. 'I will found my community. Then they will come. The king will help me.'

Huy looked at him. 'I have a last question.'

'Yes?'

'Why did you leave my house? Did you know the Medjays would come?'

Surere smiled. 'I did not need the king's guidance for that. I knew they would arrive sooner or later. I saw them watching your house and I escaped through the back. Prison teaches you cunning.'

The same covered rickshaw took Huy back to the city. Once more, Huy had no opportunity to see out, but guessed from the number of twists and turns it made that they were taking a deliberately tortuous route. Once more, he was accompanied by the taciturn messenger. When the rickshaw came to a halt, it was not at his house, but at the deserted harbour.

Huy understood why he had been dropped here, from where a large number of roads led off back to the various parts of the city, but guessed that they had underestimated his knowledge of the twisting muddle of streets that formed the harbour quarter. He had no doubt that he would be able to keep pace with the rickshaw and follow it wherever it went, even now, when the descending darkness created streets of shadow where there were none in reality, and when the eye played tricks on the heart.

The messenger moved so fast that Huy barely saw the club as it swung through the air at his throat. The force of the blow caught him squarely and sent him sprawling, gasping for breath, temporarily blinded, rolling in the dust. Spitting and spluttering, forcing his flailing hands and knees to get a grip on the earth and push him back upright, he heard the rushing creak of the rickshaw's wheels and the patter of feet as the haulier sped off into the night.

By the time he had got to his feet and turned round, the square was empty again. Evidently Surere's caution was still one step ahead of his madness.

Huy wanted a bath, to wash the fatigue away, and put some order into his thoughts. It seemed several days since he had seen the girls' bodies in their mockery of repose at the embalmer's shed that morning. As for Surere, Huy had surrendered to the thought that the man had left the Southern Capital long ago. The discovery that he was still here, that his heart had found time, in that sinister cell he inhabited, to entrench itself in the obsessions of his lifetime, and that he believed himself to be in contact with the ghost of the dead king, were complications Huy could have done without. He could not admit to his own heart that Surere was involved with the girls' killings; though perhaps – the dark thought was there – Huy was afraid to admit such a thing was possible, as he would then, however innocently, have played a part in their deaths.

There remained the question about whether to tell Merymose that he had seen Surere. If he were captured, the former district governor would be executed, by the cruellest method prescribed in the Black Land: impaling. Whatever their differences, could Huy hold himself responsible for sending him to such an end? He found himself glad that he did not know the location of Surere's hide-out.

Huy made his way home, but, still finding no message there, he forced himself to set off again, heading for the City of Dreams. He would talk to Nubenehem about his discovery of that morning. If he drew a positive result from his questions, he would have something else to tell the policeman, as well as the manner in which he believed the victims had been killed.

But as he walked, he became more and more convinced that he would also have to tell him about Surere. Would Merymose believe that he had no idea of the man's whereabouts now?

'Are you here for business or pleasure?' scowled Nubenehem from the couch where she appeared to live. Rolls of dark fat lolled over the little sofa's back and sides. More than ever, it seemed to have become a part of her body.

'Business.'

'I see. So, not *my* business then. My business is your pleasure. You should take some. You didn't spend any time at all with Kafy last time you were here.'

'How is she?'

Nubenehem scowled. 'She's gone.'

Huy was surprised. 'Why?'

'None of your business.'

'I noticed she was badly bruised. Was it a client she didn't like?'

'I said it's none of your business.'

'Where has she gone?'

Nubenehem looked at him. 'You're really concerned, aren't you? Well, don't worry. She's gone back to her village, near Saqqara. But not forever. She hasn't been killed, like those rich tarts the whole town's gossiping about.'

Huy felt an emptiness in his stomach. He had been concerned for Kafy; more than he would have thought, for someone whose interest in him stretched no further than his wallet.

Nubenehem was in a bad mood, reaching for her liquor jar and belching. A stale smell hung in the air. 'So, what do you want? If all you want to do is talk, there are plenty of other places you can go. Bees don't make honey by talking.'

'I want to ask you about Nefi.'

The woman's eyes became clever. 'What about her?'

'Has she been back?'

'No. Anyway, I thought you found her.'

'I lost her again.' Obviously the town gossip had not revealed who had been killed.

Nubenehem relaxed. 'There's plenty of girls besides her and Kafy. I might take you on myself.'

'Oh yes. And Min's erection's gone soft, too.'

Nubenehem cackled. 'You shouldn't talk about the gods like that.'

'About Nefi,' Huy continued, carefully.

'I haven't seen her.'

'I wondered – something about her – something you might remember.'

'You described her to me. That was her. Little slut, all puppy fat and innocence. You should have heard the way she talked. I tell you, she even shocked me.'

'But she was a good looker, wasn't she?'

'Plump little lips. Cheeky little tongue. Give a man the best kind of pleasure he'd get this side of the Fields of Aarru.'

'Pity you never saw her naked.'

Nubenehem was getting careful again: 'What are you driving at, Huy? Of course I saw her naked. She wanted to work here.'

'Did anyone else see her?'

'Couple of the clients. Whistled. Told them she wasn't on the market yet.'

'You never got her full name?'

'No.'

'One thing I'll always remember about her – that little cat tattoo just above her navel.'

Nubenehem clammed up. 'We're not talking about the same girl.'

'Oh?'

'Nefi had a tattoo all right – they all do – but it wasn't a cat, and it wasn't anywhere near her navel. It was a scorpion, and it was on her shoulder blade.'

'Oh,' said Huy, certain of Nefi's identity now. 'Can't have been the same girl then.'

He turned to go, but halted at the door.

'Where did Kafy get that bruise?'

'I told you – '

'I know. None of my business. But I've got friends in the

police now. Merymose. Heard of him? I could get you closed down. Who was that client I saw in here? The richly-dressed one who paid you over the odds?'

Nubenehem started to sweat, and half rose.

'Don't call out the cavalry,' said Huy. 'That'll only make things worse. Who was it?'

Nubenehem was silent, but there was a hint of fear in her eyes.

'You put on a show for him, didn't you? A special show. With Kafy. That's how she got that bruise. And that's why she's left. She didn't want any more. But you don't have a licence to operate that kind of brothel. Now, who was he?'

Finally the fat Nubian looked at him. 'Don't give me any trouble, Huy. We've known each other for a long time.'

'Who was he?'

'You can have any girl you like, free.'

'Who was he?'

She spread her hands, but her look was defiant. 'All right! He was someone from the palace compound. I don't know why he decided to come here, but they do, now and then, and he paid well. You're right. Things got out of hand.'

'His name.'

'He didn't give it.'

Huy was not sure if she was lying or not, but she read his thoughts and continued, 'Even if I knew it I wouldn't give it to you – and you may have enough clout to shut me down, but even Merymose couldn't reach high enough to touch him.'

'What did he do to Kafy?'

She spat out the words. 'Nothing. He just watched.'

SEVEN

'With a needle?' asked Merymose, intrigued.

'Yes. Or something similar. A very fine knife, perhaps, or even an embalmer's chisel,' replied Huy.

'But how can he have done it? There wasn't any sign that any of the girls struggled.'

'What do you think?'

Merymose spread his hands. 'That they didn't want to struggle?'

'Yes.'

'Do you mean they were drugged?'

'It might have been simpler than that. They might have trusted him.'

'What, to stick a knife in their heart?'

Huy shrugged. 'They might have been embracing. Perhaps the furthest idea from their hearts was that they were going to be attacked.'

'But why?'

'If we knew the answer to that!'

'But there might be no motive at all. Where would that leave us?'

'Oh,' said Huy. 'I think there's a motive. However strange it is, I think there's a motive.'

'The only thing that's consistent is the way these girls have been killed.'

'There is much more,' said Huy, convinced that Merymose must have seen the other similarities too. 'They all come from similar backgrounds, they all live within the palace. They're all the daughters of rich officials. They're all the same age. They all had . . . a look of innocence.'

Merymose looked uncomfortable. 'But what about their characters? Iritnefert was a firebrand, but she hadn't *done* anything. Neferukhebit, well, if what you say is true . . .' his voice trailed off.

'I think it's true. The brothel keeper had no reason to lie to me, and I've talked to the other clients who saw her there.'

'How could she want to do such a thing?' Merymose's voice was harsh.

Huy looked at him. 'You have been through enough to know what this world is like.'

'I think of my own daughter. She never had a chance to grow up, either.' Merymose looked at Huy. 'I am going to destroy this spawn of Set.'

Huy had delayed telling Merymose about Surere, waiting for the right moment to come. Now he wondered if he had left it so late that he would arouse the man's enmity. There was something else. Merymose clearly had orders to ignore any trail that led to the palace compound. It would be unwise, therefore, to say anything to him of what he had learned about Ipuky's sons from his first marriage, or about the other visitor to the City of Dreams. But yes, he would tell the policeman about Surere now. Then at least the responsibility would be shared.

'What about the third girl?' he asked first. 'Mertseger. What have you been able to find out from the parents?'

'Very little. They know of nothing. Certainly no lover. To talk to them, you would think she had still been playing with toys. She was their only surviving child. They were old when they had her.'

'There is something I must tell you,' said Huy, tensing himself. 'Something I have not told you, which I should have done. I should have told you days ago.'

Merymose looked at him. 'That surprises me.'

Huy squared his shoulders. How could he explain his feelings, his reservations, and the reasons for them? Would Merymose, who had been so badly let down by Akhenaten himself, be able to feel any sympathy at all? He might simply view as collusion what Huy saw as loyalty. And now there was another doubt: the new element which Surere had introduced – contact with the ghost of the dead king – was not only the one which had triggered Huy's decision to tell Merymose all he knew; but also the one which might exempt Surere from any blame. If the former administrator had gone mad, then the passion that possessed him had more to do with the re-establishment of the New Thinking in a new place, rather than any desire for vengeance. Surere, however cunning and even ruthless his instinct for self preservation made him, might also be an innocent.

If he had *not* gone mad, but was really in touch with the ghost of the old king . . . Well, there were precedents for such things; and if ever a monarch might not rest peacefully in the Fields of Aarru, that man was Akhenaten.

Huy conveyed this as best he could. For most of the time he was talking, Merymose's expression remained set. Huy found himself wishing that he were able to read some comment on the policeman's face – anger or disapproval might have been easier. To his own distress, he realised that he was in danger of abandoning his self reliance, and making a friend of Merymose.

Coming to the end of his account, he remembered the fate of the mason-overseer, Khaemhet, held responsible for the security of the prisoners deputed to him for the journey from the granite quarries to the Southern Capital. The obelisk was nearly completed, and a place had been prepared for it near the south pylon of the Temple of Ptah; the barge which had brought it had long since returned to the quarries upriver. But what had become of Khaemhet?

'He was executed,' Merymose told him coldly, leaving Huy with an extra burden on his conscience; though in this case the burden was easier to bear, since Huy, given the choice, would never have put the interests of the prisoner below those of the jailer.

'Would you recognise the house again?' was all Merymose asked.

Huy shook his head. 'It was a door like a thousand others in a wall like a thousand others.'

'A man like you might have looked through the screens of the rickshaw; might have counted the time it took to reach the place, calculated the direction in which you were taken.'

Huy took the criticism in silence. It was true that he was more than capable of all that; what was more, the measures Merymose described were ones which he would usually have taken instinctively. He had deliberately laid them aside this time, though he had not been aware of any direct instruction from his heart to do so.

'When I went to him, I had no idea that what he would say to me might bring him within the sphere of our investigation.'

'Even though he is obsessed by an ideal of innocence? Even though he sees the parents of these dead children as traitors to his cause? Even though he has spoken to you of vengeance?'

'I cannot associate what he said with the action of killing. His obsession is to form a community loyal to the Aten, away from this city. He rejects us and our values.' Huy had spoken his last words quite automatically; but their utterance made him realise in what world *he* now lived.

'We must find him,' insisted Merymose. 'I do not share your instincts. It hasn't escaped anyone's notice that a former senior official of the Great Criminal goes on the run, and at the same time a series of murders begins of the children of other former officials of the Great Criminal. Kenamun is baying for blood.'

'Well, now you have some bones to throw him,' countered Huy. 'We know how the girls were killed; that they must have known or at least trusted their killer. If it is no demon, we know that his motives are not robbery or sex. Some strange ideal moves him.'

'Some strange ideal moves Surere,' said Merymose crisply. 'My heart tells me we need look no further than him.'

Merymose did not involve Huy in the search that followed. He did not explain why, and this placed a distance between them. Huy knew that it was because the policeman could trust him only so far after his confession. He wondered how much had been passed on to Kenamun, though it was unlikely that

Merymose had told the priest everything. Merymose did not like Kenamun, neither did he trust him; and if the case were solved, Kenamun would take the credit.

But his confession to Merymose had a positive effect too, because permission was granted to the former scribe to talk to the bereaved families within the palace compound.

Huy took this to mean that Merymose still needed his help. He might be able to elicit information from the families which the policeman had missed; but he had reckoned without the gulf between granting permission to interview, and the families' readiness to talk. His own association with the court of the Great Criminal was not a secret, least of all to these people, and their attitude to him was one which Merymose had no power to influence.

'Of course I'll help,' said Taheb. 'I have been ready to ever since you began this.'

'Can you arrange for me to see the parents?'

'That will not be difficult. When?'

'As soon as possible. But they will object to seeing me.'

'Not if you come with me. And I will send letters ahead. They will not refuse. They remember favours owed to my father and to my father-in-law. I will take you this evening. In the cool of the day. Let me write the letters now. Then we will wait for their reply.'

Later, Taheb raised herself on one elbow and let her hand slide along his thigh. They lay together in the same blue-white room, though this time their lovemaking had been gentler and more familiar, as warmth and exploration of each other's bodies and hearts had succeeded the glorious frenzy of their first coupling. This time, they had not needed the stimulus of an aphrodisiac. Huy felt he could get drunk on the smell of Taheb, sinking his lips into the base of her neck where it joined the shoulder. Now, re-aroused, he curled his body to hers and slid into her lazily, as they lay side by side. They kept their eyes open, to see into one another's hearts.

Afterwards, they were washed by Taheb's body servants, and dressed in visiting robes. By dint of some speedy alterations by

Taheb's dressmaker, Huy was able to wear a kilt and shirt that had belonged to Taheb's late husband, his friend Amotju. He ran his hand over the clothes. It was a strange sensation to have them on – more intimate than sleeping with his widow.

They rode into town in her finest litter, crowded with cushions covered in a rich fabric from a country undreamed of, far to the north at the edge of the world, on the other side of the Great Green, and covered with a canopy of light linen cross-threaded with blue and gold. The messenger sent ahead had ensured that there would be no difficulty in entering the palace compound, and the guards at the gate did no more than salute as the litter passed within the walls.

'They are prepared for more than just a social call,' Taheb said. 'It will be interesting to see what excuses they offer for not having seen you before.'

'I didn't get beyond the major domos,' said Huy.

Mertseger's father, the general in command of cavalry, was a stocky man like Huy. He was sixty, and the muscle on his chest and arms had gone to flab. The gold bracelets he wore were too small, and bit into his forearms. He was lavish in his grief, his eyes still red-rimmed from tears and sleeplessness, and although he was polite to Huy, he barely seemed aware of who the scribe was. He spoke of nothing so much as his guilt at having depended only upon his own staff for security. Old Mahu, the gatekeeper who had slept on the night of Mertseger's disappearance, had been dismissed without a pension, but that action had done nothing to mollify the general's conscience.

'Had she been seeing anybody?' Huy persisted.

'What do you mean?'

'I mean a man – or any companion.'

'She had her friends, but they met during the day. They often went to the park to sit by that lake.'

'Might someone she knew have made a date with her at night?'

The general looked at him uncomprehendingly. 'Why would she go there?'

'She was found there.'

'That is what I cannot understand,' the general had turned in upon himself again, hardly aware of the presence of his guests any more. 'Perhaps it is a judgment on me.'

Huy exchanged a glance with Taheb. 'Why?'

The large, wet eyes were full of suspicion and dislike. 'Who are you, again?'

'I am trying to find out what happened. I am working for Kenamun'

The look turned to triumph. 'And do you have children?'

'Yes, but not here.'

'Distance will not save them, if you are as I am.'

'What do you mean?'

'We both served the Great Criminal.' His eyes suddenly narrowed, and he came close. 'I remember you, Huy, after all. I was in charge of a chariot division in the north. An important one. We sat in Tanis and heard the news from the coast, but we never had any orders. We were awaiting orders to move against the rebels from you, you scribes and administrators,' he spat out the words, 'in the capital. But no word came. Now we are paying the price. Five years ago my son was drowned. Now I have lost my daughter; you will lose your children, too.'

Huy felt the heat of fear. But these deaths were not caused by an avenging spirit from beneath the sunset. They could not be. He made himself remember the teaching, bringing coolness into his heart: all things have a natural cause which can be discovered. What seems supernatural is simply what is beyond present understanding. The last thing Akhenaten ever taught was vengeance: the idea was so foreign to his nature that he would never have entertained the thought. But, the general was possessed by it. The acceptance of the idea provided him with a curious salve for his guilt. Pity for his children was engulfed in pity for himself. As for his wife, the healers had given her drugs; there was no talking to her. She lay on a bed on the verandah by her daughter's door, asleep but for her eyes, which were open.

* * *

Taheb's litter carried them the short distance within the compound to the towering, dark house of the Controller of the Silver Mines. Ipuky had no illusions about supernatural intervention. A long, grey face and grey eyes reminded Huy of Kenamun, though the priest seemed ebullient by comparison with this sombre banker. The room in which he received them was sparsely furnished, despite his wealth. It looked like the chamber of an ascetic priest. However, the stiff chairs and table were made of the expensive blackwood which grew to the south and was imported from Punt. The one decoration was a finely-executed wall painting of the cobra-goddess, Wadjet, goddess of the town of Buto, in the Delta.

'I hope you realise that it is only on account of the entreaty of Taheb that I see you, Huy,' were his words of greeting. 'You are persistent. That is not necessarily a quality.'

'I want to find out who killed Iritnefert.'

Ipuky did not blink. 'I have my own men to do that. I have told Merymose what I know. Why inflict further pain on my family and myself by telling you again?'

'Because of what you might have remembered since.'

'That is the talk of one casting around in the dark,' said Ipuky with a smile like the light covering of frost which, on hard nights in the middle of *peret*, fringes the rushes on the banks of the river. He extended scant courtesy, even to Taheb, and despite his wealth his servants only brought in the minimum guest-offering of bread and beer.

'You might have developed suspicions. Perhaps your men have uncovered something. I could help.'

'We both know you are thinking about someone in particular, don't we, Huy?' There was mockery in the man's voice.

'I am thinking about no one.'

'You are thinking about Surere,' retorted Ipuky. 'These killings started when he broke free; and he did not escape punishment for working under the Great Criminal, as we did.'

Huy would not share this burden of guilt. 'Well?' he insisted, as Ipuky fell silent.

The tall man fixed him with his cold eyes. 'I do not see him as a killer. But when he is found it will be interesting to see what he has to say.'

'Do you know where he is?'

Ipuky took his drink and sipped it. 'No.' There was a long silence. Ipuky looked at neither of them. He was waiting for them to leave.

'Perhaps your wife has something to add; or your other children.'

Ipuky's eyes seemed sightless. 'My children are young. All are under seven years old. My Chief Wife saw nothing, knows nothing. Iritnefert was not her daughter. If you want to find out about her character, you must ask her mother, and she is in the Delta.'

Huy glanced at the wall painting. 'She was in the City of the Horizon with you?'

'Of course,' a hint of impatience in the voice now. 'And when the city fell and she decided that my fate was no longer one she chose to share, she returned to Buto. Do not draw any conclusions from the painting. I had it done to remind me of a mistake from which I have learnt much, and of an ending which I have no cause to regret.'

'What was Iritnefert's mother like?' asked Huy.

Ipuky turned his gaze slowly to Taheb. 'A fire that could burn in water, would you not say?'

Taheb lowered her eyes.

'And only Paheri could control it,' Huy spoke into the silence.

Ipuky was caught too off guard to conceal his reaction. He glared at Taheb.

'Did you tell him?'

'It doesn't matter,' said Huy. 'I was in the City of the Horizon. Taheb was not. What happened to your sons?'

'Clearly you know.'

'I know that Paheri stayed with your first wife, and that your second son was lost when the northern empire collapsed.'

Ipuky looked grim. 'That is true, and that is all there is to say. They are both dead now.'

'Are you sure? They were loyal servants of the old king, but they were also your children.'

Ipuky looked at him with hatred. 'They are dead to me. I do not even acknowledge them as my own.'

'What is in his heart?' Huy asked as they left. They had seen little of the house apart from a gloomy garden and a long corridor which led from the entrance hall to the room in which they had been received. All the doors off it had been closed, and the only light came from the open archways at its beginning and end.

'Nothing. Stones,' Taheb answered. Her voice was weary.

'It is a miracle a man like that has any children at all.'

Taheb smiled thinly. 'You are wrong. Look at how he described his wife.'

'What?'

'She didn't leave him because his star had fallen; she knew well enough that he was the kind of man who'd recover. But the collapse of the City of the Horizon gave her the chance to escape. He would never have let her go if he hadn't been distracted by his own interests. His second marriage is a marriage of conformity. Its children are the children of duty.'

'How do you know?'

'Ipuky's new Chief Wife is the daughter of a colleague of his. She is fifteen years his junior, and little more than a housekeeper and unpaid bedslave. She is a human letter of partnership between two businessmen. Iritnefert's mother, if you can believe it, could make Ipuky burn.'

'Why didn't Iritnefert live with her?'

'That was Ipuky's way of punishing her. And torturing himself, I think. Iritnefert looked like her mother, had the same temperament. She was also the price her mother had to pay for her freedom.' Taheb paused. 'He was lying about the painting on the wall. That is a torture, too,' she added.

'Then why does he have it there?'

'Ask the gods. They made us this way.'

'Do you think he loved his sons?'

'He only loved Iritnefert's mother. That was all the love he had to give. To others, he would give something called love; but it was only a reward for loyalty.'

They were being carried along a man-made gorge – a yellow road of sandstone flags between two red cliffs of plastered wall which sloped inward at the top, towards the building they were encircling. On them, giant painted images of the gods walked in a stately procession. The stiff representations were new. Harsh and impersonal, they had no life in them. Huy looked at them. These were not gods with whom you could speak.

At the house of the Chief Scribe, Reni's major domo was waiting at the gate to meet them. He guided them through a broad passageway flanked with heavy half-columns surmounted with lotus blooms, and protected by the couched forms of rams, Amun's beast, in sculptures larger than life. They entered a large garden, which was protected from the heat by the umbrella of a huge and ancient vine, the shadow of whose leaves dappled the paved floor. From an intricate system of pipes, water flowed everywhere, in fountains and little artificial streams, irrigating a profusion of plants, set in the earth or clustered in countless pots, whose unaccustomed variety and colour dazzled the eye. The gabbling of the water mitigated the noise of the crickets. The cool of the garden greeted you as you went in with a breath as welcome as that of the north wind at the top of a house during the season of *akhet*.

As they approached, Reni rose from his seat at a table near the large rectangular pool which was the centrepiece of what – as Huy now saw it to be – was an unconventionally asymmetrical garden. The scribe was dressed in the white garb of mourning, and his lined face looked worn. His own hair was combed out over over his shoulders, and for make-up he had used only the faintest trace of *kohl*. He was pale, but his careworn expression could not disguise the malice in his eyes.

There was cunning in the face, too. Huy could not guess by what means Reni had saved himself and his family from the debacle that followed Akhenaten's fall; but he knew many good men whose ruin had been the price the scribe had paid to be sitting here now, and the thought tempered his sympathy. He looked around for Reni's wife – the mother of Neferukhebit – wondering if she was the source of the girl's character.

If Reni remembered Huy from the past he made no reference to it, nor did his face betray the slightest sign of recognition. He motioned to the chairs around the low table, standing and positioning Taheb's himself, as servants approached with wine jars and food: honey cakes, figs and heron's eggs. Huy allowed a beaker to be filled so as not to transgress the etiquette of hospitality, but he did not propose to drink any wine. Ipuky might have saved himself, but at no one else's expense. What was on Reni's table was blood-food, and Huy would not touch it.

He tried not to let his feelings show in his eyes; but he sensed that the scribe knew them anyway. Neither of them, however, gave any sign, and indeed Reni seemed too preoccupied by his grief to give other matters much thought. But he was too intelligent not to have a conscience. Whether he was intelligent enough not to pay heed to it was another matter.

'I hope you don't think it strange of me to sit here,' said Reni. 'It was here that my middle daughter, Nephthys, found Nefi. I feel close to her here, as if perhaps her *Khou* were hovering near me.' He smiled sadly, taking Taheb's hand and squeezing it.

'What do you think happened?' asked Huy.

'I don't follow.'

'Surely my question was clear?'

Reni's brow darkened. 'My daughter was killed, here, in my own garden. No one can find out how, or why. That is what happened.'

'And that is all you can tell me?'

'Do you think I have time to play games? If there were more, I'd have told the Medjays.'

'Do you remember me from the City of the Horizon?' Huy asked.

'Yes, I do. You are working for Kenamun now?' replied Reni, mildly.

'In this matter.'

'Kenamun and I know each other well, despite our differences in the past. Nowadays, we visit each other's houses,' Reni continued, in the same mild tone.

Huy registered the threat, and Reni saw that he had, before turning to Taheb, stroking her hand as he spoke. 'Nephthys found Nefi's body early, when she returned from the house of her husband-to-be. My sons were not yet back. The gates were still open, but there were servants about.'

'Were there any in the garden?' asked Taheb, wishing she could draw her hand away. There was something reptilian about the old man's grip.

'It is unlikely. For most of them the day's duties were over.'

'So it was unguarded.'

Reni shrugged slightly. 'Taheb, my dear, I have a gatekeeper, and this house is within the palace compound. Besides, there had been one killing. No one had any reason to suspect a second.'

'But you knew that Surere had escaped. That he was in the capital,' said Huy.

Reni looked at Huy in contempt. 'The Medjay captain asked me that too, and I give you the same answer: how would an escaped convict find his way into the compound? All the gates are guarded. Even you and and people like you have to have special permission to enter.' He turned away with a dismissive, impatient gesture.

'Do you have your own men working on this?' asked Taheb.

Reni looked across at her. 'Ipuky wanted me to join forces with him, but I decided to leave matters in the hands of the authorities. I would not know what orders to give my men. But my sons . . . I cannot answer for them.'

'How did they react?' asked Huy, remembering what he already knew about this.

'The older boy is angry – but then, Ankhu is a man of action. He never learnt his letters properly, to my shame, and now he talks of the army. He hunts with the young king, so no doubt some sort of career is assured him.' Reni had not changed, thought Huy, remembering the oily modesty with which, even in the old days, he had scored social points off colleagues who he knew could not compete. 'Nebamun is more like me,' continued the scribe complacently. 'He controls his grief, turns it into a subject for contemplation. But I would not say he was beyond revenge.'

'And your daughters?'

Reni folded his hands. 'They are women.' Then he caught Taheb's eye and lowered his own with a slight cough.

He was saved further embarrassment by the rustling approach through the fecundity of his garden of his wife, accompanied by two of the children. They came towards the seated group cautiously but without hesitation – almost as if their entrance had been prearranged.

'May I present to you those members of my family who are at present – ah – available,' said Reni. 'Ankhu is at court, and my oldest girl will still be busy in the archive at the far end of the house.' Huy wondered whether that eldest daughter, who worked as Reni's secretary, had helped him destroy the documents he drew up during Akhenaten's reign, which would have given such priceless ammunition to his enemies, before turning his attention to the newcomers.

Reni's Chief Wife surprised Huy. She had a neutral, neglected look. Her mourning white was not as dazzling as her husband's, and the downward turn of her mouth appeared to be the result of permanent, not recent, grief. But her face was intelligent; out of her eyes gazed a heart which acknowledged a wasted lifetime. She should have left him years ago.

Nebamun was probably seventeen, already a man, though his face was still bright and open. Nephthys was dark, and her large features had an open attractiveness due to the personality which animated them. Physically, her looks were like her mother's; her mother's face before hope had been dashed out of her life. It was odd that there should be nothing of Reni in the features of either child.

They greeted Taheb with pleasure before turning to Huy with more guarded expressions. He wondered if they had been primed to talk to him, and how far they had been told they could go. He longed for the chance to talk to each of them in private, but saw little hope of it.

Huy found himself unable to know where to begin. Merymose had asked the questions of fact, at a time when they were all too stunned by the event to react other than practically. The questions of theory and of hypothesis seemed wrong now, and looking from face to face, he wondered how much good the answers would do him. To encourage himself as much as anything, he ventured a handful of general questions about Neferukhebit's activities on the days leading up to her death – questions which resulted in conventional answers, the activities of any rich young girl marking time between the end of her education and the arrival of her husband – for these girls were on the fringes of the royal household, and work – such as Taheb did – was taboo to their class.

Ankhu and Nebamun would have it easier, but for the majority of privileged men work was a nominal activity as they laboured more or less intelligently in the upper ranks of the army, the civil service and the priesthood; most of the graft was done for them at a humbler level. The boy was quieter than his sister, and gave tongue-tied answers. His sister's death seemed to have affected him more deeply, though he bore himself with a kind of frightened dignity in front of his father.

Talking to Nephthys was a way of getting to know her dead sister by proxy, for she had plenty of spirit, and within her there was a streak of rebellion against her family, particularly her father, though there was no hint of it in any word she spoke. Nephthys was younger than her brother, but seemed older, and more sure of herself. Her independence was further underlined by an impending marriage, news of which she now shared with Taheb. Marriage, though it was to be to a priest, and thus well within her world, represented an escape from her family. Huy wondered what the husband was like. Would Nephthys turn into her mother in time? From what was being said, perhaps that was unlikely. Though the marriage had been arranged, Nephthys would be the man's first wife, and he was near her own age.

Throughout the interview, Reni kept a Horus eye on proceedings, interrupting, when he felt an irrelevant question had been asked, with the speed and precision of a young judge. It was a relief when a secretary appeared – sent by his oldest daughter – and summoned him away on business that had to be decided that night. He left with reluctance; but his departure did not make conversation any easier. Huy had the impression that a body servant was lurking somewhere within earshot, to report any indiscretions back to Reni, and that everybody knew this.

It had grown dark, and the night, for the season, was unpleasantly close. After a short time, Reni's wife excused herself, and everyone stood, watching her wend her way through the small jungle, looking lonelier than ever as she went. An awkward pause followed, and Huy, feeling that he had learnt all he could, made no attempt to continue the conversation. He had one question left, and he wanted to put it to one or other of the children alone. He hoped that only one of them would accompany Taheb and himself to the door, and he hoped that person would be Nephthys. Whether Taheb had divined this, he did not know, but as she rose to leave, she linked arms with the girl, and turned towards the gate.

'Good night,' Huy said to the boy. 'Don't worry. I'm sure your sister can see us to the gate. And thank your parents again.'

'I will,' replied Nebamun. There was an appeal in his eyes which Huy could not read.

As he was leaving, the boy seized his elbow, bringing his face close.

'Where can I find you?'

'I live in the harbour district. Taheb knows.'

'All right.' The strong hand let go of his arm, and Nebamun stepped back.

'Goodbye,' he said again, in a clear voice.

'Goodbye.'

Huy watched him retreat and then followed Taheb and Nephthys, finding them talking softly at the gate. Nephthys, her arms folded, leant on the jamb, her hair softened by a halo of light from the gatekeeper's lamp. Her clear face betrayed no grief or anxiety at all. The door stood open and beyond it on the pavement was cast the shadow of the Medjay posted to keep watch.

'Nephthys,' said Huy, drawing her aside. 'Where did your sister get the tattoo?'

The girl looked at him in wonder. 'What tattoo?' she asked.

'She had a scorpion tattooed on her shoulder.'

The girl's eyes became even wider, then she suppressed a laugh. 'That was just like her. I'm sorry, you must think I have no feelings at all. But I admired her. She was the only one who stood up to him.' She laughed again. 'I can't believe it! He'd have killed her if he'd known.'

'But didn't he see the body?'

Nephthys looked at him. 'I'm certain he hasn't seen one of us naked, ever. I don't even know how we got to be born. My poor mother has slept alone as long as I can remember.'

'What about his other wives?'

'He doesn't have any. Nor any concubines. He spends nearly all his time, day and night, with Iryt, my big sister. They have an office at the far end of the south wing.'

'Why didn't she join us tonight?'

Nephthys shrugged. 'She's always busy. Even we never see her.' She looked at him. 'You can draw what conclusions you like from that. I just can't wait to get out of this house.'

'Do you hate it so much?'

'I'd have married a boatman to get out.'

'Why?'

She was about to answer, but the gatekeeper approached, giving Huy a suspicious look.

'Time to close up,' he said sourly.

Nephthys smiled at Huy a little sadly. 'I'm counting the days. Goodnight.'

They did not talk much in the litter on the way back to Taheb's house. Huy was wondering how much truth there had been in

113

what Ipuky had said about his sons. Taheb's skin still crawled from the scribe's touch.

'His poor wife,' she said, finally.

'It seems he prefers the company of his daughter Iryt.'

'Sometimes neglect is worse than abuse.'

'Then she should leave him.'

'How can she? What would she do? Her only hope is widowhood.' She was silent for a moment. 'And now she's got to bear the death of her daughter. Why do you think Reni said that no one had any reason to suspect a second killing?'

Huy looked thoughtfully out through the curtains of the litter at the night sky, bright in the silence with the light of a million stars.

EIGHT

The search for Surere, the first of its kind ever to be conducted by the Medjays, had been organised with precision by Merymose. The Southern Capital had been divided into eight segments, like slices of the round, flat loaves the Semite guest workers baked, each segment's inner edge bisecting one of the main quarters of the town, into which it was split by the two main thoroughfares, one running north-to-south, and the other east-to-west, which met at the centre. Most police were concentrated in the crowded districts of irregular streets, such as the harbour quarter, and special details were dispatched to the privately-run brothels which did not fall under the control of the priesthood. Nubenehem, her peace made with him, complained of this bitterly to Huy; the attentions of the Medjays had cost her a day's profit, with the following day well below average on takings, as frightened clients stayed away. Following an instinct based on Huy's description, for what it was worth, of the house where he'd met Surere, Merymose sent Medjays out of uniform – another innovation – to the good residential districts.

All of which led to nothing. Not even the raids on the town's three gay brothels brought forth a whisper of information about Surere's whereabouts, and after four days of intensive hunting, over ground which included the Valley of the Great Tombs on the west bank of the river, Merymose began to think that perhaps, after all, the escaped *political* had done as he had told Huy he would, and left for the northern deserts to found his religious community. The thought came as no relief to Merymose, for although the loss of his quarry might not mean his dismissal from the Medjays, he could expect demotion, or at best to end his days in no higher rank than he held now. He reflected gloomily on the price of his ambition, because he had gone out on a limb to persuade a mistrustful and increasingly hostile Kenamun to consent to the operation he had mounted, and then he had only achieved it by linking Surere to the serial killings.

If it were now fixed in Kenamun's mind that Surere was the killer, another murder would be all that would save Merymose's neck. And yet he had been thorough, efficient, and ruthless in his investigation, not drawing the line at torture to extract information where he thought it might be withheld. But a new thought struck him – another murder might lead his superior to assume that Surere was, after all, still hiding out in the Southern Capital, and that, too, would hardly be to Merymose's credit. Merymose had not been left much by life apart from his career. Now it looked as if that, too, were coming apart.

Surere could not disappear in the way that he had without powerful help. Merymose had to find out where that help came from, but he told himself that he had no reason to suspect Huy of withholding any more information. The risk would certainly not be worth it to the little ex-scribe.

The tail end of the search for Surere was still in progress when they found the fourth girl. She was near the east bank of the River, five hundred paces south of the town, lying on a flat white rock where the crocodiles could not get her, though by the time she was discovered by a Medjay patrol at the sixth hour of day when the sun was at its highest, the vultures had eaten her eyes and part of her face, and the flies were so glutted that they could not leave the feast unless they were picked off. As the season progressed, so had the heat, and Huy and Merymose stood over the body with their heads wrapped in linen cloths to protect them from the sun.

'We had better get her away from here,' said the Medjay healer, removing the last of the flies and quickly wrapping the corpse in a linen sheet before any more could settle. 'That is, if you want her examined before she falls apart.' He turned away to supervise his two assistants, who manhandled the small bundle on to the back of a covered ox-cart.

As it drove slowly away towards the town, so the small knot of idlers and gawpers dispersed, back to the quays and the eating houses to tell about what they'd seen, and Huy and Merymose were left alone.

'What do you think?' Huy asked him, as they looked at the rock. The flies had returned to cluster on two small lakes of dried blood, all that remained here to show where the girl had lain, apart from the lingering smell.

'It's the same, isn't it? Except that the body wasn't found soon enough. I don't envy the embalmers.'

'No.' Huy was pensive. He had told Merymose nothing of his thoughts about Ipuky and Reni – sensing the policeman's disappointment and mistrust when he told him that he had been able to find out no more than he had himself. All his reservations were based on intuition, supposition. He had nothing to give Merymose to take to Kenamun, and the priest-administrator would not thank him for information which cast suspicion on two of the most powerful men in the country. At the same time, the more he delayed, the greater Surere's danger was.

The girl's body had been laid out just as the others, and it had been the work of a moment to discover the tiny stab wound under the soft left breast.

'I've sent men into the palace compound to find out which household she was from.' Merymose was tense. 'The outcry will raise Set. I must find the man who did this.'

Huy stooped to pick something off the ground, that lay three-quarters hidden in the rough yellow grass that grew around the sides of the stone. It reflected the sunlight dully in his hands, dangling from a broken chain. It was an amulet of Ishtar.

By the eighth hour, all the Medjays sent to the palace compound were back. No one had been reported missing. Not a servant-girl; not even a slave, though the enquiries themselves had stirred up panic.

117

'Are they sure?' asked Huy.

'Certain. I would not be mistaken over this,' replied Merymose shortly.

'One household overlooked would be enough.'

They had received the reports in the Place of Healing, where the body lay in the courtyard, protected from the flies and the heat by wet wrappings, waiting for someone to claim it and give permission for an examination to begin, before it was taken to the embalmers. By the twelfth hour of day, as the sun sailed west and inclined towards the horizon, finally allowing the north wind to bring its cooling relief, still no one had come.

'If we don't look at her now, we won't get a chance at all,' said the Medjay healer, who had returned and partially unwrapped the body. 'I've dressed the eye-wounds but the rot has started. If no embalmers collect her tomorrow, she must go to the lime pit.'

'Is it still light enough to work?' asked Merymose, standing, and walking across to the doctor to look down at the body.

'Yes. It will be an hour before Nut swallows the sun.'

Merymose glanced at Huy. 'Then I think we should begin.'

'And if her relatives turn up?' said the doctor.

'Then I will explain,' replied Merymose, with a confidence he did not feel. However to take no action would be worse than to risk insulting the dead.

A faint noise, like sighing, was brought into the courtyard on the wind. Merymose looked around the darkening corners, wondering if it was the girl's *Ka*. Would it object to this treatment of its old dwelling before the proper rites had been observed? The doctor, covering his nose and mouth with a cloth and summoning an assistant, carefully began to unwrap the body, supporting it in his arms like a mother or a lover. He laid it back on the table and went over to another, producing a small leather bag from his kilt. Laying it on the table he opened it, and took out a selection of fine flint knives.

'Don't worry,' he said wrily, noticing Merymose's expression. 'The spirits respect me; I have had to do with the dead for a long time.'

118

'These dead are my responsibility,' replied the policeman. 'It might have been possible to prevent this.'

'You did what you could. The dead know us; they know what is within our power to achieve and to prevent.'

Huy bent over the body silently. The damaged young face had been beautiful. A high forehead curved back gently into a rich tangle of dark, curled hair; she had an aquiline nose, full, sensual lips and a proud chin. The teeth were unusually white; strong and regular.

The assistant lit torches at her head and feet, and the light from these outlined the contours of her dark skin.

'Would you say that this is her natural colour?' he asked.

The doctor came over and looked. 'It is sunburn,' he said finally. 'I had not noticed.'

Huy had taken one of her hands in his, running his thumb across it.

'Feel this,' he said to Merymose, who had come up in turn. The policemen could see that the skin was rough, and the nails, though diligently polished, were chipped and broken.

'Perhaps, in the struggle,' suggested the doctor. He held a slender knife aloft. 'Now, if you would just give me room.'

What struggle, thought Huy and Merymose simultaneously. There should have been no struggle.

'Just a moment,' said Huy. Then he looked at Merymose. 'Her feet.'

There was no need to touch them. The soles were hard, and the edges of the big and little toes carried a rind.

'Look at the anklet,' said Merymose, suddenly. Huy did so. It was made of copper.

Huy grabbed one of the torches and brought it closer, careless of the wax dripping on to the dead skin. The girl wore no other jewellery – now, at least; but he noticed that the long lobes of her ears were pierced, and that there was a slight graze on the side of her neck. There were other, dark marks on her shoulders and sides. He turned to the doctor questioningly.

'Bruises, of course,' said the healer. 'I told you there had been a struggle. She'd been badly beaten up, poor kid. Three ribs are broken. Now, if you'll let me get to work while there's still light, I ought to be able to confirm what I suspected when I first saw her – ' He paused, bending over the body, a long hardwood implement in his hand. Breathing through his mouth, he manipulated his probe between her legs. After a minute, he straightened up.

'What is it?' asked Merymose.

'She was raped. In both the nether gates. But she was no virgin before it happened, if that's of any interest to you.'

Huy produced the little amulet of Ishtar from the linen pouch at his belt. He looked at Merymose. 'This should have told me more, earlier.'

Merymose returned the scribe's gaze, telling himself once again that there was no reason, surely, to distrust him.

An hour later, standing in the darkness, so far from having the fourth murder in a series, they had a new killing: one which was superficially like the others, but whose only real resemblance lay in the infliction of one particular wound, and the manner and location in which the body was laid out after death. The girl, whoever she was, despite the aristocratic looks and fine body which had at first misled them, would only have found houseroom within the palace compound as an under-servant.

'It's much more likely that she was a whore,' said the doctor, having washed his hands and arms, and rewrapped the body. 'She wasn't clean enough to have been a harem girl. But it's hard to imagine what she did to deserve a fate like this.'

Her sunburnt skin and her rough hands and feet made her poor. The copper anklet was probably the only thing of value she had possessed, and it was curious that it had not been stolen, for all metal was valuable in the Black Land. It was the little amulet which told them most about the girl. The cult of the goddess Ishtar had come into the Black Land with settlers from the far north-east where the Twin Rivers flowed. But the settlers had been courtiers, the sons and daughters of kings and dukes exchanged in marriages which formed part of peace treaties between the Black Land and the Nation of the North-East. The cult had remained after those who had brought it had embraced the gods of the Black Land, the true gods, the gods of the land in which they now lived, but it remained as no more than a fashion among the rich. It was a fashion now past. Only among the poor, the retainers who had accompanied their masters and later fallen from favour, or among the half-caste children brought up by superstitious mothers true to their old faith, did the little goddess of love and war retain a true following. There would be few such people in the Black Land now. Huy hoped that the discovery would ease the task of finding out who the girl had been.

'Why do you think she was killed?' asked Merymose as they made their way from the Place of Healing to Kenamun's office.

'I don't know. If we knew why she was killed in that way we would be closer to the truth.'

'It's simple. He's becoming violent.'

'Did this girl struggle; make him lose his temper?' Huy said, and then had another question. 'But why change the *kind* of victim? This girl was poor and sullied.'

'Do you look for reason in madness?' asked Merymose.

'I thought we were dealing with an obsession.'

'But why copy the method, if this time the killer is someone else?'

'Who knows that there is a method to copy?' said Huy quietly. 'Only a very few people.'

'Only a few that we know of,' said Merymose. They fell silent. Then the policeman continued, 'If the method was copied in order to make us believe that the crime was committed by the killer of the other girls, then our new killer is either clumsy, or stupid.'

'Or clever.'

'What?'

'If the method was copied, whoever did it *intended* us to think that it had been copied clumsily and stupidly. Perhaps there are not two killers, and this has been done by our man to confuse us. In which case we may be closer to him than we think.'

Merymose shook his head. 'You are burying yourself in too many thoughts.'

'Yes,' said Huy. 'We must stay on one path, while being aware in our hearts where others may lead. But I am not sure now that we seek Surere for this.'

Merymose's eyes became veiled. 'How can you say that?'

'You still think I am protecting him. If I knew where he was, perhaps I would still try to. I tell you this because I know that I cannot expect trust if I do not give it. But Surere could never make love to a woman. He could never penetrate, not even if his life depended on it, for he is sure that their nether mouths contain teeth, and that once his limb was inside them, they would bite it off.'

'And that is why he prefers the company of men?'

'Can you think of a more compelling reason?'

There was a speck of yellow phlegm on Kenamun's lower lip. As he spoke, and this lip joined the upper, so the wet dot transferred allegiance, and then back again. Huy found himself looking at the man's lips alone, and the spittle switching from one to the other, in horrified fascination and to the exclusion of everything else.

Kenamun was in a white rage. Although he fought to control it, his voice trembled, and the knuckles of the hands which clutched the chair at whose back he stood were huge, the skin stretched tautly across them. His dark eyes were glassy with fury, the pupils dilated, the whites bulging in their sockets. A lock of hair had worked itself loose in his wig and now hung over his forehead. He could not have been aware of it, for it was the only untidy thing in the room, a banner of disorder in the midst of the most rigid ranking. His simple, expensive tunic hung straight, without the least sign of a crease or a sweat stain, despite the heat of the day and the advanced hour of morning. The jewellery at wrist and neck shone as if it were still on display in the shop from which it came, and the odour from the man was simply – nothing. A sense of freshness, perhaps, but no smell either personal nor scented.

'I want Surere caught and brought here; and I want him tried and executed, and I want this before the next public rest day,' he repeated.

'There is no proof that he – ' said Merymose.

'Do not speak to me of proof. You have advanced nothing – *nothing* – to suggest that he is not guilty, apart from the theories and musings of Huy, whom I was ill-advised enough to allow you to engage as consultant.' Froth bubbled at the corners of Kenamun's mouth. He licked it away with a flick of his tongue, sucking and swallowing.

Huy knew better than to speak. He remained where he was, standing behind Merymose and a little to one side, head bowed, but eyes surreptitiously up, on that obstinate morsel of spit, now stretching into a thin line of glutinous liquid string between the two lips.

'One who was a *colleague* of the escaped criminal. I do not now deny that I hoped he would lead us to him. And now what do I learn? That he met Surere and withheld knowledge of the meeting from us. He is lucky that he confessed his action before we discovered it, for that is all that has saved his life.'

Huy darted a quick look at the back of Merymose's head. The Medjay captain had no doubt been forced into the minor act of betrayal which consisted in breaking Huy's confidence to Kenamun, and there may have been political or strategic reasons for it; but the act had raised a wall between them. There was no reason why Kenamun should ever have known about his meeting with Surere. Perhaps now Merymose was beginning to share Kenamun's desire for an arrest at any price, so long as it was soon. But if Surere was not the killer, then the murders would go on. Huy could not believe that Merymose could not see that. Kenamun clearly hoped to reap the rewards of a quick and flashy double solution, and to have moved on to other work before the murders recommenced.

'This fourth murder confirms the escalating violence of the man's mind. He is deranged. He cannot have gone far. I want him found, I want a confession extracted, and I want him executed!' Kenamun repeated deliberately. 'You have until the next rest day. Bring him to me and I will make sure he talks.'

Merymose did not reply. Huy looked at the black polished surface of the table behind which Kenamun stood. The ink holder; the leather pad for papyrus; the serried ranks of brush pens and rolls of paper, a cylindrical pot containing bronze pins and a paperknife. From them his gaze travelled to the hands on the back of the chair, noticing a red mark the shape of a new moon on one of them, noticing the heavy turquoise-and-gold ring of office on the middle finger of the other.

Kenamun had come to the end of his tirade, and now as his expression relaxed Huy thought he could discern something behind the anger in the man's eyes: an expression so fleeting that he was not able to identify it, but one which left a disturbing impression on his heart. But now Kenamun had begun to speak again.

'There is of course no question of retaining the services of this man. You say that he has contributed materially to the progress of your investigation. I do not accept that he has contributed anything that we could not have found out without his help. Your faith in his expertise was ill-founded, and does no credit to an officer of your rank and experience.'

Merymose started to say something.

'You are forbidden to work in association with him any further. Is that clear?'

Merymose was silent.

'*Is that clear?*' On his dignity, Kenamun was beginning to sound increasingly like the petty official made good which he was at heart. Huy looked at the over-long face, the ridiculous beard, and realised with a sudden shock that the man was scared. But of what? Was Horemheb beginning to lean on him? If so, he might well be frightened for the sake of his future ambitions.

'River-horse dung,' said Merymose, when they were outside. The sun glared down, dazzling them. Neither had slept, and both were shabby from the long night. In addition to which, Kenamun had taken care to keep them waiting an hour in an unventilated antechamber before seeing them. Huy said nothing, resisting the urge to ask Merymose why he had told Kenamun of his meeting with Surere, and wondering if the Medjay would give an explanation. But none came. They walked northwards, towards the town centre.

'The man is river-horse dung, and deserves to be rolled into a ball for scarabs' eggs.'

'Perhaps his masters aren't pleased with him either.'

'Then they should remove him.' Merymose looked at Huy. 'I threw you to the crocodiles to save my job.'

'Then you are river-horse dung too.'

Merymose drew himself up. 'You will be all right. Your work will not suffer.'

'And what do I get out of this?'

'I will indent for a fee for you.'

'To whom? Kenamun? Don't hide behind officialese.'

'You don't know how lucky you are not to be part of the system.'

'If it weren't for what you've been through, I'd break your jaw.'

Merymose stopped. 'You don't believe I would have sold you short for no reason at all, do you?'

Huy looked at him. 'Do you still think I am holding back on Surere?'

Merymose did not answer quickly enough. Huy started to walk away, realising with bitterness how far away he still was from being accepted in this new society, and realising to his renewed surprise how much he wanted to be. Was this engagement his ticket to respectability, and is that why he had accepted it? How would Taheb react to this debacle? But what irritated him above all was the jumble of loose ends he would be obliged to leave behind, just at the moment when he was beginning to see how to unravel them.

He heard the Medjay come up behind him. 'Look,' said Merymose. 'I still need your help. If you want an apology, you have it. But don't let me down now.'

'Do you mean you want me to track down Surere?'

'I want to find the killer. I don't want to hand a scapegoat over to Kenamun for him to torture into confession.'

Huy smiled guardedly. 'But we can no longer work together.'

Merymose returned the smile. 'Not openly. But I am a match for Kenamun, and you are forgetting our mutual friend.'

*　　*　　*

Huy returned home to bathe and sleep. He awoke towards evening, put on fresh clothes and took himself out to one of the modest eating houses that lined the bank of the river on either side of the harbour. He ordered black beer and fig liquor, bread, pork and *persea* fruit, sitting outside under an awning and looking at the boats. Most had already lit their fore-and-aft lamps, which twinkled like glow-worms in the gathering dusk. A large cedar-barque rode at anchor, still loaded with its expensive cargo and guarded by two men armed with spears and swords. Near it were two smaller barges, being made ready to make the short journey upriver to Edfu to collect another load of sandstone. A handful of people crossed the harbour square, dawdling on their way home or to drink after work. The city was clean, quiet and contented. Around him in the eating house a few other diners sat, chatting quietly, and from the next table came the muted click of the pieces being moved by two players of twenty-squares. Looking south, Huy could just make out the shape of the wall surrounding the palace compound, and remembered that quiet and contentment existed in reality for very few, and then only for a fraction of the time one spends under this sun. Beneath the surface of this gentle evening a complex and never-ending game, which had something in it of a duel, was being played, the players swimming in their milieu like fish, at different levels which they would occasionally switch, to make an attack or to retreat, to seize prey or to threaten. The dead sat around the edge of the game and watched, knowing the secrets.

Banking, despite his better judgment, on Merymose's promise, and unable to shelve the curiosity which had been awakened, Huy pushed relaxation aside with his stool and made his way from the eating house back through the harbour quarter towards the City of Dreams. It occurred to him as he walked that he had not seen Taheb since their visit to the palace compound. Might she be expecting him to visit her, or at least to send her a message? It gave him a qualm to realise that a large part of his need to see her again stemmed from her usefulness to him as a go between. He desired her too; but she had not lit a fire inside him as Aset had. He did not flatter himself that he might have had that effect on her, but he did wonder what course their liaison would take.

Nubenehem looked up as he pushed the door open. She was not alone. Standing by her table was a black-skinned girl from the far south, eyes and teeth dazzling white; breasts and buttocks mirroring orbs. Apart from gold chains around her neck, waist and ankles she was naked. So firm and perfect was her body that there was something unearthly, even unsexual about it. She shone in the lamplight like the black wood from Punt, and might have been carved from it.

'Tell me you've come to spend some money,' said Nubenehem in greeting.

'I'm still earning it.'

'What about this one?' The fat Nubian nodded at the little girl from the south, who primped and giggled. There was a freshness and gaiety about her which lit up the brothel, making it appear dismal by comparison.

Huy smiled at the girl. 'At any other time . . . But now I need one more favour.'

'You want to sell me the wig back? No.'

'A valuable wig like that? Are you joking?'

The black girl laughed and skipped away behind the curtain which led to the interior of the City of Dreams. She seemed possessed of an inviolable grace. Huy wondered how long she had been in the capital, and how she had got there.

'What favour?'

'I'm looking for a girl.'

'Another one? What's wrong with the ones I've got?'

'This girl's from the Land of the Twin Rivers.'

'Oh,' said Nubenehem sarcastically. 'Easy. You sure you only want one?'

'She might have gone missing from wherever she works.' Huy tried to pick his words carefully, but Nubenehem was on the defensive immediately.

'A place like this?'

'Yes.'

'When?'

'Two days ago. Perhaps three.'

'You still working for the Medjays?'

'No,' he told her truthfully.

'Good. Didn't seem like your style, somehow.'

'Have you heard anything?'

'How fast do you suppose news travels?' Nubenehem remained cautious.

'There aren't that many girls from there.'

'I'll ask around. See if anybody's lost one.'

'Thank you.'

'It'll cost you two silver pieces.'

Huy stepped out into the warm night, smelling the heavy, dusty odour of the air appreciatively. Still rested, he was disinclined to return to his solitary house, and although the thought of visiting Taheb came to him, he rejected it. He wanted tonight to himself, and the idea of the wealthy formality of her house oppressed him.

He returned to the quayside, content for a time to walk up and down, allowing his thoughts to marshal themselves. His eyes wandered from object to object; the façades of the buildings with their dark, secretive entrances, the boats again, the glitter of the restless water, the fishermen's lights out in the middle of the stream, the faces of the other people taking their evening stroll. Again he found himself wondering how much contentment there was behind any one among this sea of faces; but the pursuit of such reflection was vain. For most of those around him, life was a simple matter ordered by the pharaoh and the gods, by the annual rise and fall of the River and the three seasons, by the narrow strip of green in the desert along which they existed. Complexity was neither necessary nor desirable; it was of no practical use and it solved nothing in the end.

Someone touched his elbow so timidly that he thought it had been accidental, until the gesture was repeated with more insistence. Now he turned and saw Nebamun walking beside him.

'Hello,' said the boy, looking at him with hollow eyes.

'Hello,' replied Huy, not slackening his pace.

They continued in silence for several paces, part of the crowd and lost in it. Few people were talking and the silence of night cast its pall over the city. The occasional cry of laughter, or a voice raised in anger, seemed shocking, like a violation. But the silence was not complete; it never was, here, for there was always the insistent murmur of the river and the laborious, unending sawing of the crickets.

'Do you have a message for me?' said Huy finally, recognising that the boy looked to him to break the silence.

'From whom?'

Huy spread his hands. 'I don't know. From your father?'

'No. What would he have to say to you?'

'That is true.' The thought of Reni sending any sort of word to him amused Huy; but the boy continued to look at him seriously.

'Then what is it?' Huy asked after a moment longer.

Nebamun hesitated before replying. When he spoke he looked ahead, only occasionally glancing at Huy, though whether for approval or in anticipation of an interruption, Huy could not tell. 'We heard today that Kenamun has sacked you. We heard because Kenamun and my father are friends. Business associates. Colleagues. You know. A finger in every pie.'

'Yes?' Huy would not be drawn into criticising either Reni or Kenamun. Life here had taught him that much caution, strongly as it ran against his nature.

'I believe he was wrong to do so.'

'Do you?'

'Yes. Aren't you angry?'

'He wasn't satisfied with the work.'

'Are you going to leave it – just like that?'

Huy looked at him, but there seemed to be nothing to read in the face, beyond a curious anxiety, and a curious devotion. 'I have no choice.'

'But can you bear to?'

There was an insistence in the voice which irritated Huy. What need did he have to justify himself to this pampered youth? But then that thought was replaced by another: was not there agony in Nebamun's voice as well?

'It is not a question of what I can bear, but of what I have to put up with.'

Nebamun licked his lips and swallowed. 'If you cannot find out who killed my sister, no one can.'

'What about your brother Ankhu? I thought he had plans.'

'Ankhu is good at starting game. He is not good at stalking it.'

The crowd milled around them. Huy took the boy's arm and guided him through it, to the edge of the quay, where a short, broad jetty jutted out into the water. Resting a foot on the bollard, he faced Nebamun.

'Now we can speak in more comfort. What do you want?'

'I want to help you.'

Huy smiled inwardly. After so long alone, now he was surrounded by people eager either to enlist his help or offer theirs.

'You cannot.'

'Why?' There was a touching air of innocence about the boy.

'Your father would not approve. Kenamun would not approve. It would be bad for me. In any case, I can have nothing more to do with the investigation.'

Nebamun looked at him defiantly. 'I cannot believe that you are the kind of man who can just stop working on something, leaving it half-finished like this.'

'What do you want from me? I earn a living the way I have to, not the way I choose to.'

'But don't you care about the people? Don't you want to put an end to this?'

'The Medjays will do that.'

'The Medjays! They are donkeys.'

'No, they are not.'

'I do not believe that you will simply drop this case.' Nebamun spoke more quietly, but his tone was desperate.

'Because you do not want me to. But you must trust Merymose. He knows what to do.'

'Let me help you.'

'I am sorry. There is nothing to help me with.'

The boy fixed him with a final look, but said no more, and slipped away into the crowd, only turning back once more. Huy wished that he could unravel the message in his eyes. Might there have been a challenge there?

He waited impatiently for news of Surere's capture. Kenamun's deadline came and went, but Taheb, with her ease of access to information, heard nothing to suggest that the Medjay captain had been either dismissed or taken off the case.

Huy assumed that he was still working on it. He spent his nights with Taheb, but these days he had begun to notice the glances the servants gave him, and made excuses when she wanted him to join her dinner guests. The role they were casting him in was clear, and he hated it. Sensing this, Taheb sought to reassure him, but his own pride stood between them, and they both knew that their affair had more to do with simple pleasure than deep feelings. Their lovemaking was still passionate, but the tree had lost its spring leaves, and under the summer foliage there was no sign of fruit. A hint of duty had crept into their relationship.

At last Nubenehem had news for him. Huy handed over the fee she had demanded.

'I should have asked you for more,' said Nubenehem. 'You're getting some real stuff for your money.'

'What is it?'

'You'd better not tell anyone where you got this from, or I'll have to move my business to Napata,' said Nubenehem, seriously. 'And if that happens, I'll see you fed to Sobek's children.'

'I've no wish to be crocodile fodder.'

Nubenehem grinned. 'She was called Isis.'

'Original.'

'Not her real name. I don't know that. But where she worked might interest you.'

'Yes?'

'At the Glory of Set.'

Nubenehem had named a specialised brothel for a clientele which enjoyed inflicting and receiving pain. There was something else about it. It was a place for the very rich, indirectly managed by the priesthood, within the walls of the palace compound. For some time a rumour had persisted that Horemheb, in his moves to clear up the corruption which had flourished like rampant weed during the years in which the city had fallen into neglect, had more than once attempted to close it; but that the interests which protected it were still too powerful for him to dispense with.

Huy would need Merymose's help if he were to proceed in that direction. He thanked the fat Nubian for her help – it had indeed been well worth the two pieces of silver she had demanded – and left.

He was at the end of his patience when a message came from Merymose.

'I'm not sure that I enjoy being your go between,' said Taheb, as she delivered it.

'You aren't,' said Huy, reading the note. It was hurriedly written on a scrap of papyrus which had been used and scraped clean several times before. Taheb watched him.

'You can't wait, can you?' she said, drily.

'What?'

'To be back in action. You have changed, Huy. You are a very different man from the frightened little scribe who arrived here a year ago.'

'Have I offended you?'

'Why?'

'There is something in the way you speak.'

She clasped her hands, and took a few short paces. 'I feel shut out.'

'There is no reason for that.'

'Can't you leave this alone? Isn't it becoming dangerous? What if Surere knows you're after him and decides to do something about it?'

'What makes you mention him?'

Taheb made a gesture of impatience. 'But he must be the man you're after. Perhaps he is working for someone else. You suggested that he must have powerful friends. In any case, the closer you get, the more likely you are to be killed.'

Huy smiled. 'No one is going to kill me.'

'That is a stupid remark.'

Huy spread his hands. 'I cannot stop working on this just because it is dangerous. You know that.'

'You do it simply because the mystery fascinates you.'

'That is part of it. But also I want to stop a bad thing.'

'To protect us from it?'

'Yes.'

'All of us, in the Southern Capital?'

'Yes,' Huy said, wondering what this was leading to. Taheb's look was ironical.

'But you do not care for us. What do you care for this society? It is corrupt; it has betrayed the ideals you worked for, and it has robbed you of any position.'

'There are still good people in it. As for the rest, if I am to survive myself I must adapt to what time brings.'

'Why don't you leave this to the Medjays?' she asked, suddenly changing tack.

'It is they who asked my help.'

'Look,' she said, finally, exasperated. 'I see this taking you away from me. I do not want it and I do not understand it. Leave it. I have a boat ready and it will take us to the Delta. Let Merymose deal with this.'

'I cannot let him down. What do you want me to do, ignore this? If so, why did you let me have it? You could have lied to me.'

'Your heart is too like a maze. It is as twisted as the entrance to a tomb.'

They looked unhappily away from each other. 'Do you use this as a means to get away from me?' she asked finally.

'No,' he said; but he was no longer sure, and he knew his voice betrayed his thoughts. Taheb, however, only heard the tone that she wanted to hear.

'But you will not come with me to the Delta?'

'No.'

She sighed, her eyes bright, but her dignity intact. 'Then I will go alone. I want to see my children. Write to me when this thing is over. Then perhaps you will know what you want to do.'

'Do you know what you want to do?'

She relaxed, smiled. 'I do not. Come, we are grown and we talk like children bickering over gleanings.' They embraced, but knew that it would go no further. Not this moment, and perhaps not ever again, despite the time it would still take to confront that knowledge. The heart loves security, at almost any price, and for most men it parts company reluctantly, slowly, and selfishly.

'If you cannot find another way to be in touch in my absence,' said Taheb, 'use my steward. He is my cousin, and can be trusted.'

Their spirits had parted, and though their bodies stayed together for a while longer, it was the first time since they had met that they found it difficult to talk. As he left, though he did not like to admit it to himself, Huy felt his sadness tempered with relief. There was little time left before his meeting with Merymose, so he did not return to his house, but took a circuitous route which would bring him to their rendezvous at the moment the sun touched the top of the western cliffs. For a while as he walked, faster as the sun began to dip more quickly towards Nut's receiving mouth, he thought he caught a glimpse of someone following him; but it was no more than a glimpse, and the figure – a ghost in a dark robe – slipped out of sight behind a building's corner before he could even take in its size. After that, his senses remained strained and alert for several hundred paces, but there was no more hint of a shadow, and as he moved away from the busier streets he became increasingly confident that he was alone.

As the sun began to set, so the darkness and the light divided into separate, intense pools. The dusty streets, now that the traders had withdrawn from them, seemed to enjoy a silent life of their own. At the end of a shaft of light streaming down an alley which led to the river, a scorpion dozed on a broken brick, though at Huy's approach the little brown statue bristled, pincers and sting instantly alert. The sounds he made fell into the embrace of a dead echo, and he felt that he might be the last man on earth. He was walking past the barley granaries now, three rough structures of tamarisk planking. A watchman squatted at the entrance of one, but he was asleep, and might as well have been a statue. Near him two other guardians of the granaries, cats, lay curled at the perfect centre of twin outcrops of shade.

Another twenty paces along and around a corner, a fourth granary stood. Its door, as expected, was ajar, and after checking the street Huy quickly slipped through it into the twilit interior. The barn was not full, but in some of the stalls on either side of a broad central aisle he could see heaped mountains of grain as his eyes became accustomed to the dark. There were the long-handled wooden shovels used for transferring the food into sacks, and at the end of the aisle there rose, like the bulk of a god's statue in a temple, a wooden hopper, its side bound with bronze. It was a huge thing, hanging in the air from a beam, its duct turned to point down over one of the stalls. As he approached, Huy could see that the duct had been opened, for the flax rope which controlled it was pulled down. Smelling the fresh dust in the air he realised that the load of grain in the hopper had only recently been discharged into the stall.

The wide door of the stall, which the sackers would open outwards when the time came to make use of the grain within, was bolted shut. As Huy came closer, he noticed something glinting in the half light, not quite halfway up the door and towards its centre. Suddenly his heart beat faster and he quickened his pace, in the grip of dreadful panic. The dull reflection came from a gold finger ring. Four fingers were thrust, gripping, through a gap between the planks of the door. Huy touched them. They might have been made of stone. He recognised the ring.

He turned round in an instant, but the silence of the granary mocked him: he was alone. Pulling the heavy bolt of the door, he stood back to allow the weight of the grain to open it, then, working with frantic haste, swung it wider, and, grabbing one of the shovels, began to dig. He seemed to be moving through mud, his actions hampered as if in a dream. He slipped and stumbled on the grain, sinking into it. As fast as he dug, more tiny oval ears tumbled into the hole he had made, in their thousands. But at last he reached the body.

Merymose lay on his back. Barley filled his eyes, his nostrils and his mouth. His fingernails were broken and bloody from when he had thrown himself at the door and torn at it, in the moment when he realised that he had been shut into the stall, and what was going to happen next.

NINE

'Why? Because Kenamun has lost his best man, and I have no faith in his ability to solve this on his own. Nor, to judge from their efforts, do I see that I have much more to expect from my own people. You will get all the help you want, though I suspect you will be better off working alone. I will pay you in whatever goods you request, at the rate of half a *deben* of silver a day. I will allow you twenty days. If you have not solved this by then, you will be dismissed. If you have, I will buy the house you live in and give it to you.'

Huy looked round the bleak room, unable to believe he was in it again. He had spoken to no one about his discovery of Merymose's body, not even to Taheb, who was distracted by the preparations for her reluctant departure, and had not questioned him when he told her that Merymose had not appeared at their meeting place.

The news of the policeman's death came soon afterwards – the sleeping watchman had found the body when he made his evening rounds. But by that time Taheb had already embarked.

Huy had returned to his house in order to work out a way of getting into the brothel known by the impious name of the Glory of Set – Nebamun had been right, he found that he simply could not let the whole thing drop, and now there was a friend's death to be avenged – when the message had come for him from the palace compound.

'I am waiting,' came sternly from the other side of the table. But was there an unsteadiness in the voice? Was Ipuky as sure of himself as he seemed?

Huy looked across at the Controller of the Silver Mines.

They were both sitting, this time, though the man's austerity had relaxed very little further than that. What he was offering was something which Huy had hoped for, though the source was surprising. He looked into the severe face again, noting details. Lines at the corners of the mouth indicated that it might have smiled once, but there was no doubt that the eyes were anxious. There was no sign of grief for his daughter, but then, the house was in a state of permanent mourning.

'What made you approach me?' Huy asked him.

'Merymose was not a fool; and you made a good impression when we first met. Now; your answer.'

'I accept.'

'Good. Not that you could have refused.'

'Oh?'

'You need the work. More importantly, you need Merymose's killer. Thirdly, if you had refused, I would have told you I intended to point out to Kenamun that the door of the stall in which Merymose was found had been opened. The significance of that doesn't seem to have occurred to him.'

Huy said nothing.

'He's a clever man,' continued Ipuky; 'and as devious as a politician needs to be. But he isn't a detective.'

'There is something I must ask,' said Huy.

'Yes?'

'I do not know if you will like it.'

Ipuky sat back, folded his hands, and looked at Huy questioningly.

'I need to know more about you.'

Ipuky's face tightened. 'How is that necessary?'

'You want me to find Iritnefert's killer.'

'You find that unnatural in her father?'

'No. But I imagine you know what is said about you.'

'What is said about me,' repeated Ipuky drily. Huy could not tell the thoughts behind the words. There was a long silence before Ipuky continued, 'What is said about me should not concern you. I am content to let you form your own judgment of my character. Not that my motives should bother you.'

He made to rise, in order to conclude the interview. Huy

knew at once that he was entering territory that was dangerous and interesting. He kept his own voice even.

'That isn't enough.'

His interlocutor raised his eyebrows a fraction, but remained seated.

'I cannot proceed at all without your cooperation, and without your trust I will have no light in this darkness.' Huy did not say that he was not prepared to exchange trust for trust with Ipuky. Hiring Huy would be a very effective way of keping him under observation, and neutralising the effectiveness of his investigation. But why would a man like Ipuky go to such lengths, when, if he felt that Huy was a threat, he could so easily have him killed?

'You'd better ask your questions,' said Ipuky sourly, after a pause.

'I want to talk to you about your children.'

'I have already told you, they are too young.' But one runnel of sweat began to trickle down his forehead from under his headdress.

'I mean Iritnefert's brothers.'

Ipuky sighed, flexing his hands as they lay at the edge of the table, and was silent for a long time.

'They are dead.'

'Are you sure?'

'Yes.'

'Then why are you so worried?'

At last Ipuky met his eye. Now he made no attempt to banish his feelings from his face. 'Because I am *not* sure,' he said at last. 'You obviously know about my sons. I do not know how I can have fathered such children. No one will believe this, and I know exactly what the town says about me, but I loved Iritnefert. I am a man who destroys the women he lives with. My first wife left me, and she was right to do so, but I kept the child I cared about from her. Since I married again, I have had more children, but my second wife has turned into a shadow.' He fell silent, looking into himself. Huy waited.

'To my little children I am a shadow also. Even to myself I have become hollow.' He spread his arms. 'The blows life deals

139

you make you stronger; but there comes a time when, if the blows do not stop, they begin to weaken even the strongest.'

'Your sons?'

'They are my punishment; but I do not know what I am being punished for. Why did Osiris have Set for a brother? Is it possible to carry evil within us, like a disease we transmit but like to think we do not suffer from ourselves?' Again he paused, wearily, but now that he had started to talk something like relief entered his eyes and his voice. He wet his lips and swallowed before continuing.

'I do not like to mention their names. To speak them perpetuates them. But I must. Three years separated the boys. Paheri was the older, poor Menna the younger. I had such hopes for them, and was even pleased when, at the age of seven, Paheri asked to enter the priesthood. Of course it was too early in his life to be certain that the gods had called him, but I could have wished for no better career for him than that of a priest-administrator. His resolve did not falter. But there were other things. When he was ten, he caught his younger brother stealing dates. For this transgression, he . . .' Ipuky's voice faltered. 'No, I will not tell you. Menna was never well in his head or heart – Tawaret did not smile on his birth, and the torture he experienced at his brother's hands pushed him forever into a lonely land inside himself . . .' Again the gaunt man broke off. The room seemed to have become darker. Huy did not move.

'Paheri never once looked at a woman, though of course by thirteen we were hoping to match him. At first we thought he would grow out of his phobia. Two years later, he entered the priesthood, attached to Surere. They stayed together throughout the reign of the Great Criminal, until the end.'

'What happened?'

'Paheri had a row with him. Paheri was furiously jealous. Of anyone. Of anything. Above all, his dislike of women developed into a hatred. Woman had contaminated Man ever since Nut first bent over Geb. That was the image that obsessed him: Nut, bent over across the sky, swallowing the sun, trapping Geb under her. I believe Surere encouraged him in this. His mother was the only exception. The woman who had let him out of the darkness of the birth-cave into the light.'

'What happened to Menna?' Huy spoke into the silence.

Ipuky looked up at him. 'I think he is dead, now. For a long time I was afraid that he had survived the raids of the Khabiris on our last outposts in the north; but an infantry captain who had known him managed to make his way back to the Southern Capital and contacted my steward. He handed over a ring and an amulet that I recognised. I had given them to Menna when he first left to take up his post. He seemed to recover considerably after Paheri left home. I had to try to give him a chance to be independent. The job I found him was an undemanding clerical one. The governor was an old acquaintance, who knew of my son's shortcomings.'

'And Paheri?'

Ipuky's voice was calm. 'He believed in the Aten ferociously. When it was certain that the City of the Horizon would collapse, and all that it stood for, I wrote to him, to try to get him to save himself. He returned my letter spattered with his own blood, and a reply. In it he told me that the blood he had spilt over my traitor's proposal – his own blood – was nothing to the blood of the traitors that he would shed if the Aten fell, and it was his lot to take vengeance.'

'There was nothing but love in the teaching of the Aten,' said Huy quietly.

'There are causes, and there are warriors for causes,' replied Ipuky, his voice as empty as the desert.

'Why do you think he is here?'

Ipuky looked at him again. 'Because of the killings. I want you to find him.'

'But Iritnefert was his own sister.'

'You do not know my son.'

There was a long silence, during which neither man looked at the other.

'I will need free access to the palace compound. I will need to be able to go anywhere without being stopped,' said Huy at last.

'See my quartermaster. You may wear my livery. That will

guarantee that the guards at the gates let you through. I will tell my steward that I am taking you on to the staff as – ' he paused for thought for a moment '– as a tax consultant. The assessors will be working on last autumn's crop soon enough, and the job will ensure that no one in the household asks any questions. You will also be able to come and go without anyone feeling the need to see you receiving direct orders from me.' He gathered his robe about him. 'And now – '

'There is one last thing,' said Huy.

Ipuky returned to his seat. 'Yes?'

'I need access to the Glory of Set.'

'What?' said Ipuky, sharply.

'To the brothel, the Glory of Set.'

Ipuky sat back. 'I do not know what you are talking about.'

Huy was taken aback. Why should Ipuky tell such a transparent lie? Ipuky must have read his thought in his eyes, for he quickly qualified what he had said by adding, 'I do not see how that can have any bearing on who killed Iritnefert. Surely, after all I have told you, you must see that.'

'Let me explain.'

The tall man leant forward, hands clasped, an expression of anxiety suddenly naked again on his face. 'Surely you are not suggesting that my daughter –? I know she was a wild spirit, but – '

'No,' Huy reassured him. 'I do not think so. But there may be a connection.' He explained, briefly, about Isis.

'I have never been there, and I do not know who does; but it is powerfully protected,' Ipuky said wearily. 'You must forgive me for not being more helpful. For some years now I have not been much in society. I have preferred books and silence for company. In any case, what excuse could I possibly invent for you to go there?'

'Nevertheless, I need to go. There are questions I must ask there.'

Ipuky looked scornful. 'And do you think they will answer them?'

'If they are paid.'

142

Ipuky shook his grey head. The dull gold in his headdress shimmered as it caught the light. 'They will never tell you. They are already paid, more than any bribe could tempt them, to be discreet. The clients of that place are among the most powerful men and women in the Southern Capital. Even Horemheb has failed to have it closed.'

'Maybe I can find a lever for Horemheb to do so. And if I can, then it would be a lever you could hand to him.'

'I am no longer interested in politics,' said Ipuky. 'But I am interested to see where your cunning takes you, and you must do anything you think necessary to stop the horror that has begun. Come back tomorrow at this time.'

Huy stood up, bowed briefly to his new master, and made for the doorway. As he reached it Ipuky called to him once more.

'You think I am as cold as stone,' he said. 'Many do. That is my protection. But I must know who killed my daughter. Find him, Huy, and when you have, bring him to me. Death would be too kind an end for a man who has done what he has, and I do not want him to escape into it.'

The Controller of the Silver Mines laid his arms on the table in front of him and clasped his hands together, sinking his head. Huy looked down at him and fired a last question: 'Have you seen Surere?'

Ipuky looked up, but his face remained rigid. If anything was detectable there, it was surprise. 'I had done with him years ago.'

'Perhaps he has not done with you.'

'Awaken us from this nightmare, Huy. Soon.'

'I will,' said Huy. Ipuky's confession had lit a bright torch in the dark labyrinth of his investigation.

Since Merymose's death, Huy had carried a dagger. It was an old thing he had had for years but only recently learnt to use, taught by one of the boatswains in Taheb's fleet. Its blade was two-edged, and made of heavy bronze, the grooves chased like lotus stems. It was fitted into an antelope-horn hilt carved at the top with the Beast's head. That night, when he awoke in the full certainty that someone else was in the room, he reached for it, where it usually lay by his headrest; but he had barely moved before he felt its point at his throat.

'You have a lot to learn,' said Surere's voice in the darkness. Huy could feel his breath, and smell the mint he chewed to sweeten it.

'And you have learnt much,' replied Huy.

'In prison, if you do not learn stealth, you die.'

'Why are you still here? What has happened to your mission?'

The pressure of the knife at his throat relaxed. 'The king will not let me go.'

'Is it he who is keeping you safe?'

'No.'

'Who is?'

Surere laughed softly. 'Light a lamp. But keep the wick low.'

Huy struck a flint and the lamp spread a tight circle of yellow light, so deep that it drew objects into it. Surere's face was sucked forwards. It was thinner, and the eyes were sunken; but they were alert, and burned brightly.

'Why have you come here again? You risk much.'

'I need to talk. There is no one but you in this city.'

'There is your protector.'

Surere laughed drily.

'How else can I think you have survived here untraced so long?' Huy persisted.

'The search for me has died down. They think I have gone.'

'Well, it is none of my business now.'

Surere's eyes darted over his face. 'What do you mean?'

'I was never your hunter, Surere.'

'You think I killed the girls?'

'Did you?'

'I wouldn't tell you. But perhaps I desire to make my peace with the man who did.' Surere laughed again. 'Under our laws, you can die for killing a hawk, a cat, or any other of the Sacred Animals. But why not kill a child if it is for the child's *good*? Tell me, Huy. I am confused by what the king tells me in dreams, and I need your help. The Aten was clear; but now I no longer know. I am confused between vengeance and salvation.'

Huy raised himself on one elbow. 'What are you saying?' He wanted to turn the lamp up, to see the man's eyes better. Jailed shadows flickered on the walls. Above all, he wanted to get up, but Surere still held the knife close to his throat, and every muscle in the man's body was taut. He truly had the supernatural alertness of the hunted.

'The age is evil. After the light, there is darkness. What is the use of continuing our race if it is to go on in darkness?'

'Is there any other way to bring us back to the light? I thought that was the purpose of your mission.'

Surere's eyes wavered, unsure. 'Perhaps the way is lost.'

'Who has told you that?'

'No one.'

'Has the king spoken to you of this?'

'Stop it!' A dry sob broke from the man's lips before he brought himself back under control. 'Forgive me. I have tried all my life to live in Truth. Now I no longer know where I am.'

'Who is the king? Who is it that you really see?' Huy asked softly, after a pause.

'I have told you! Our king! Akhenaten!'

'You have seen him again?'

'Oh, yes.'

'Where do you see him?'

Huy saw that he had pressed too hard, too fast. The cunning was back in Surere's face. 'Why? Do you want to take him from me? You are working for them now.'

'I work for no one.'

'Do you think I don't recognise Ipuky's livery? What's your game?'

'I have to eat.'

'So you compromise,' rejoined Surere scornfully. 'At least you have chosen a good man.'

'But he abandoned the Aten to save himself, like the others.'

'And what have you done?' said Surere. 'I have been thinking. I have been too quick to condemn, where in time I might redeem. You did not know Ipuky before?'

'No.'

'He was much in love with his wife. She ran rings round him, but he loved her all the same. And when she left, he clung to her shadow in their daughter.'

'And maltreated her?' Huy was still not sure how he would have answered his own question.

'I cannot believe that.' Surere's eyes had changed again, cloudy in remembering.

'You talk of redeeming,' said Huy, gently. The point of the dagger drooped towards the floor. Huy looked at Surere. He was taller than Huy, and labour had made him sinewy; but he was older, and his guard had dropped. Now was the time to take him. But if Huy overpowered him, what then? He would have forfeited the fragile trust Surere had put in him, and if he turned him over to Kenamun, he would lose all trace of the delicate thread that seemed, somehow, to link Surere with the girls' deaths. Kenamun would use pliers and the needle to destroy what was left of balance in Surere's confused mind, and then extort a confession.

'Then you cannot have killed,' Huy continued.

'But it would not matter if I have. Death is a redemption, too, if it saves the innocent from corruption.'

Huy felt the world close in on him. He seemed to be sitting at his own centre, in the innermost room of his heart, as he heard the words. The two men, forced by their fate into this intimacy that was not intimacy at all, sat in silence, the words used up. In the end Surere stood up.

'Do not follow me, Huy,' he said with his old authority.

'Tell me who is protecting you.'

Surere smiled. 'Someone who owes property to the king.'

Huy looked troubled. 'You are going, and I do not know if I have helped you. I do not even know if I should.'

'You should turn me in; but then where would you be? Do not attempt to follow me.'

Surere put down the knife, turned his back, and made for

the steps. Huy listened to him descending them, then the soft creak and click of the door. After that, night wrapped him in silence.

Getting Huy into the Glory of Set had forced Ipuky to take his steward into his confidence. The simplest method was to send Huy as a client. He would wear private clothes and say that he was a merchant from the Northern Capital. Expensive jewellery and make-up completed the display of wealth, though it made Huy self-conscious and uneasy.

The place was constructed on the same plan as the City of Dreams, though its decoration and furniture were richer. No one had questioned him or seemed suspicious. He was led from the neutral entrance hall by a quiet, equally neutral young man, who might have been a civil servant, into a room in which the walls carried friezes that depicted the perversions which the brothel traded in. As his eye travelled over them, the trepidation which Huy had felt turned to contempt, and then to pity, for here were nothing but sorry fragments of imagination.

'Please choose,' said the young man, indicating the walls.

'Choose?'

'What you would like to do. Or would you like to watch? Some do, at first, to get them in the mood. One of our best customers *only* watches.' The young man managed to combine collusion with the antiseptic disinterest of a nurse. He stood too close to Huy for comfort, invading his space. Huy could smell the sweet perfume of the oil he used on his hair and face.

He looked at the walls again. People were depicted in neat rows, engaged in activities which belied the formal expressions on their faces. The first scene showed a pair of children whipping a tied girl, perhaps their nurse. In another, an elderly woman forced a pronged implement into the anus of a muscular man wearing the mask of Horus. Further on, a young couple, tied back to back, were threatened by three creatures carrying torches. A little girl was shown twisting fish-hooks into the penis of a man suspended from his wrists by bronze wire, and in a fifth scene a man and a woman on all fours were yolked together, drawing a miniature cart, whipped by a dwarf charioteer.

'I'm looking for a particular girl,' said Huy.

'Aren't we all?' replied the young man with a crispness bordering on impatience. Huy felt anger rise into his mouth, but he made himself remain calm as he described the dead girl from the land of the Twin Rivers.

'Never seen one like that,' said the man promptly. 'What did she do? Hurt or get hurt? Or maybe you like a bit of both. Now – '

He did not finish the sentence. Huy had grabbed him by the throat, lifted him from his seat, and slammed the back of his head against the wall with a force that cracked the plaster. A small portion of the scene showing the couple with the cart flaked away and broke on the floor. Blood dribbled from the man's mouth.

'Just tell me when she left,' said Huy. The man spat in his face. Huy held on to the thin throat until the face above it turned blue and tears appeared. When the neck started to stretch, and the eyes gaped, he relaxed the pressure.

'Tell me.'

The young man, no longer so neutral, his wig awry, gasped and coughed for air.

'. . . doing my job . . .' he managed to get out.

'What job?' Huy tightened his grip.

'No.'

'Then tell me.'

Limply, the young man did so. The girl had arrived from somewhere in the north early in the season. She seemed, in his words, to have some experience of what they required, and they put her through her paces. Huy found that, during much of what he had to listen to over the next few minutes, his only defence against the temptation to break the young man over his knee was to invoke the Horus within him.

'And when she left?'

'It was unusual. There's very little goes on here that is true. Some of them really enjoy it, but mostly it's acted. So it wasn't as if she was being maltreated.' He looked at Huy half-apologetically, cringing, as if he feared another blow. 'But then we heard that she'd been killed.'

'Beaten, raped and stabbed.'

'That didn't happen here.'

'Who were her clients?'

The young man's face froze. 'Who are you?'

'Vengeance,' said Huy, meaning it, but speaking the word before he realised how theatrical it must sound. He had reckoned without the effect of his anger and his appearance on the man, who trembled. For a moment there was silence, punctuated, from somewhere deeper inside the building, by one long, isolated scream of pain.

'Did Horemheb send you?' asked the young man, finally.

'Yes.'

'I don't understand. The people who come here are powerful. Their delights hurt no one. Why shouldn't they indulge them?'

'Horemheb understands that he cannot touch you – yet. But he would not want you to think that he had forgotten you. Who were her clients?'

An unpleasant expression slunk on to the young man's face. 'I do not believe you are from Horemheb. My masters and he understand one another now.' He gave a curt signal with his head. Huy realised too late that the man's eyes had switched direction to focus on someone behind him. He did not see his assailants. He was taken from behind by two men who pinioned his arms and pitched forward into the room, the young man darting out of the way to allow his saviours to smash Huy against the wall in his turn. He felt his teeth scrape against the plaster, then someone caught hold of his hair and pulled his head back. He had a close view of one of the pictures painted on the wall that he had not noticed before. Now, in a moment of crisis, he took it in with startling clarity. Two elderly men were crouched over a naked girl who was strapped face down to some form of wooden rack. Using sharp needles and ink, they were in the act of tattooing something on the girl's back. One worked while the other watched, clutching his grotesquely enlarged erection.

The work was almost complete and the result was clearly visible: curled around the apex of the left scapula was a small, crudely-executed scorpion.

'Not the wall,' he heard the young man's voice say. 'There's been enough damage done as it is.' They pulled him round and beat his head against a stool until his brain boiled. Then blood swam before his eyes and there was blackness.

TEN

On the eve of her wedding, they found Nephthys dead. It was unusual for her to have been alone then, but she had asked for time to herself. Although the ceremony itself was a simple one – a private exchange of shared intentions in which the most important formal element was the document which laid down precisely who got what in the case of divorce – it was nevertheless going to be used by both sets of parents as an excuse to throw a party, during which they would vie with each other in largesse, showing off their wealth as well as arranging useful introductions for their unmarried children.

Huy, recovering from the wounds he had received, and cursing the broken left forearm which the doctor at the Place of Healing had put in a splint and then bound too tightly, heard about the killing from Nebamun, who awakened him early in the morning – about the eleventh hour of night – with a furious hammering at his door. Although his eyes were red, the young man seemed calm – until Huy handed him a cup of beer. His hands trembled so violently that he was unable to bring it to his lips. It took him several minutes before he could talk.

The plump girl, who had been so full of life, was killed in the same way as the earlier victims. She had been found lying on her back, hands folded, naked. There were no marks or signs of a struggle, and the body was without a blemish.

'I have lost two sisters now. I know you are working for Ipuky, but you *must* let me work with you. I have a right. I seek vengeance.'

'And Ankhu?'

'He is organising his own hunt.'

'Why do you not join him?'

'Because I think you know what you are doing.' The reason,

151

as Nebamun gave it, fell too pat. 'Won't you tell me how much you have found out?' continued the youth. 'I am older than the king; and grief has made me a man.'

Huy thought about Reni. What was the old scribe's reaction? Where would his philosophical attitude be now? Would he continue to be prepared to leave the matter of investigation to the Medjays? And what would his heart tell him about the gods, who had singled him out for this fate? Whom would he blame, and to whom would he turn for protection and comfort? His youngest daughter was almost ready for burial, her body emptied, dried out, repacked, decked out for the long night, bandaged in the finest linen with the scarab placed over her heart, and laid in her case of painted cedarwood. Soon her mouth would be opened by the lector-priest and her purification ministered by the *Sem*-priest. Horus would restore her five senses for the Fields of Aarru. She would descend to the Hall of the Two Truths, and go before the Forty-Two Judges. Then Nephthys would follow her, and instead of standing, as a new wife, before Renenutet and Tawaret, would go as a shadow to meet Anubis and Osiris.

Would Reni seek consolation in the arms of his last daughter, or would he lose himself in wine? Perhaps there was another route he would choose – after meeting the scribe again, Huy had little doubt who the rich client at the City of Dreams had been, and knew why his profile, fleetingly glimpsed, had seemed familiar. He thought of the bruise on Kafy's shoulder. Did the rest of his family know of his predilections? Nephthys had not. How might Ankhu react if he knew?

The new death showed that the killer and his motivations had not changed. The death of Isis may have been an aberration, or it may have had nothing to do with the others. That Merymose had died because he had discovered something important enough to threaten the killer was clear, and Huy knew that his own reluctance to take the policeman into his confidence had been one indirect reason for his death.

One detail needed confirmation, and Huy knew that he would not be able to perform the task himself. Even Ipuky could not arrange for him to see this body, and he no longer had the cachet of officialdom with which to browbeat the embalmer. Could he expect Nebamun to do it for him? And yet the best form of relief for this boy whom grief had made a man would be in action.

He made his decision quickly.

'I accept your help,' he said.

Hope came into Nebamun's eyes, and with it eagerness and desperation. Fear too. What secrets were there in Reni's family? Would involving Nebamun put him in any danger? But it was too late to retract.

'I need to know how Nephthys died. There is no trace on the body of a wound? Just as Neferukhebit? It will be difficult. You will have to look carefully at her body.' He decided not to tell the young man where to search.

Nebamun looked at him. 'I have already done that. I knew that there had to be a wound: she had not been drowned or strangled or poisoned. There is a little mark, only just larger than a needle might have made, under her left breast.'

'I see.'

'Is that how the others were killed?'

'Yes.'

'What happens now?'

'Go home. Comfort your parents. Find out all you can about what Ankhu intends to do. Our quarry needs very careful stalking.'

Nebamun left. Huy watched him cross the little square in front of his house and disappear around the corner on the way back to the palace compound. He thought of the forsaken wedding preparations, of the thoughts running through the head of the betrothed man, whose name he did not even know, of the decorations which were now mockeries. We establish order and think we are in control; then Nu throws over the table and breaks what we have taken a lifetime to construct. Perhaps one day he will even manage to destroy the pyramids we have built in defiance of his chaos. But however solidly we build, our lives remain huts of straw and mud, at the mercy of the River and the Sun, thought Huy.

* * *

Dressed in the quiet livery of Ipuky's staff again, make-up covering the worst of the bruises on his face, his arm tied in a linen sling, Huy spent the next two days sending himself on imaginary errands in the palace compound, which took him past Reni's house often enough to be able to assess the state of repair and height of its walls, the number of gates it had, and which streets they led into. The walls were in good condition, and smoothly plastered so that it would be hard to climb them, and if anyone had tried to, scuff marks would surely have shown where. There were two gates apart from the main entrance: a small one which led directly into the garden from an alley along the east side of the house, and a double gate for waggons and chariots opening on to a broad square which faced the north wall.

In the course of those two days no member of the family left the house. Ankhu, with well-muscled arms oiled to show them off to their best effect but with a stomach that was already turning soft, had accompanied the narrow cart pulled by a white ox which took Nephthys's body, wrapped in a white linen sheet, to the embalmer, but that was all. Huy had followed him. After he had left the embalmer, Ankhu went to the East Barracks and spent the afternoon drinking with cronies there, returning as the *seqtet* boat of the sun sailed towards the Horizon of Manu, stopping only to buy mint and coriander from a stall, and several cupfuls from a waterseller.

There was no sign of either Reni or his wife, or of the eldest daughter. Nebamun made no attempt to contact Huy. There was a steady stream of visitors to the house, of whom Ipuky was one.

'It is curious,' Huy's employer told him later. 'Reni has aged. He has shrunk, as if he were already preparing to return to Geb. I spoke to him, but he barely noticed me. The brothers are bent on vengeance, especially the older one, but he does not know what to do. He asked me if his men could work with mine, but they are a wild lot, cadets, and I do not think they will do more than relieve their feelings by scratching at the surface of this thing. They will drink, swear oaths, and plan great deeds.

If they find Surere they will tear him limb from limb.' Ipuky paused. 'Nebamun is quieter. Do you know him at all?'

'No. I met him once.'

'He is intelligent, but I cannot fathom him. The mother and the daughter have grown in stature. They have become the strength of the family. The girl especially, though there is a bitter satisfaction on the mother's face – as if a prophecy she expected were finally being fulfilled. But I fear for them. You must find Paheri and stop him.'

'Are you sure you know nothing more? I can only track the beast by watching the place where he last killed.'

Ipuky looked hard at Huy. 'I know you do not trust me completely, and why should you, when all I can offer you is a conviction that my son is here? But my spirit senses his presence.' He slapped his hands on his thighs in frustration. 'If I were you, I would have little faith in hunches either.'

The panic which had seized other parents in the palace compound had revived with new strength. Horemheb issued a proclamation that Kenamun's investigations would soon bear fruit, that no more than ordinary security precautions need be observed. The season was progressing, and every day that passed was hotter. Soon it would be *akhet*, the time of Inundation, though the river was not expected to rise as much as was hoped. If it dropped even a fraction below the minimum limit, a year of famine would follow. The people were restless. Things were not going well. Where were the gods, to aid them in their distress? Or was this the beginning of a Judgement?

'What is Kenamun doing?' Huy asked.

'Horemheb is making him sweat. He wants to deploy his full force here. There will soon be two men on every street here, and consequently none in the harbour quarter, where crime will double. There is talk of using soldiers too. But there are others who say that Surere has called forth demons, and that men will be no use against them. Kenamun himself looks calm, but there is always sweat on his lip.'

'If Surere is still in the city, they will find him.'

'Yes.' But Ipuky looked thoughtful.

*   *   *

On the third day, Nebamun and Ankhu left the house at dawn together. Huy noticed immediately that they were unarmed. The sunlight filtered into the ochre canyons of the streets through a clinging mist. A pair of egrets, unsettled by the noise of the garden gate entrance clicking shut, left their perches high on the wall of Reni's house and wheeled round towards the river. Huy, who had taken up residence in a small upper-room at Ipuky's house, where the younger children came to stare at him curiously, had risen at the ninth hour every night – well before the sun came up – and stationed himself in a doorway on the square to the north of Reni's house, from where he could look down the alley and cover the large rear gateway. The main gate was always attended by a gatekeeper, and it would be impossible to open the big northern gates unaided, so Huy guessed that anyone wanting to enter or leave the house unnoticed would use the garden entrance; but the alley was too straight and narrow to admit any hiding place. Kenamun's additional Medjays were due to be on the streets from that night, and the authorities had made no secret of the fact, in order to calm the people. Huy had argued that if there was going to be any covert movement from the house it would be now.

Early as it was, the square was not empty. Already servants had been down to the harbour and were returning with fish – their own food, for the lords who lived here would never stoop to eat cursed meat. The servants would breakfast on *ful*, olives and white cheese before preparing more sumptuous meals for their masters – dates, pomegranates, honey cakes, and, in the palace itself, rare *depeh* fruit, still imported from the lost northern empire. Walking through the mist, the sun casting thin shadows behind them, moving in silence, they were like the population of a dream.

The brothers walked south along the alley, purposefully and without conversing, turning west at its far end, the dispersing mist swirling behind them. Huy could see that Ankhu carried a packet wrapped in vine leaves. The scribe followed at a good distance. He was hampered by his damaged arm and he knew that if Nebamun saw him, he would recognise his stocky figure instantly.

As they walked through the streets and squares of the palace compound, now heading north again, the number of people about increased, and it became easier to maintain the pursuit. At the same time, Huy had to follow more closely, to avoid losing them in the crowd. He was also considering what he might do if they split up, though his heart had turned over the possibility that Nebamun had contrived to accompany his brother. A column of soldiers marching towards the palace cut Huy off for a long minute as they blocked a square, but by now Huy was sure that Reni's sons were on the way towards the city itself, and, continuing in that direction, he soon picked them up again.

Using a large ox-cart loaded with clay storage jars as cover, Huy managed to keep out of sight crossing the open space which separated the palace from the town, but neither brother seemed aware of being followed. They took the main road which bisected the Southern Capital on its south-to-north axis, and turned right, into a street which led gently up a low hill. This was a residential district, and still quiet, but Huy knew that the streets here were arranged in a grid, which made it easy to keep one corner between him and his quarry. The disadvantage was that each street was alike. The only aspect the houses presented to the road was a blank wall, punctuated by doors at irregular intervals, which led to courtyards, though you could see an occasional small upper window.

Huy had been following Nebamun and Ankhu successfully for five minutes, memorising the number of left and right turns they had made since leaving the hill road, when he suddenly knew where he was. He slowed his pace as he approached the next corner, and turned it with caution.

There, as in a wall painting, stood the house. He was sure it was the house, though he had barely been aware of it at the time. Now he could see that the original whitewash had turned pale beige. The blank brown door was peeling. High in the wall there was a small, shuttered window. Otherwise the wall was unbroken to the tiled roof and for twenty paces in either direction.

Ankhu knocked on the door and almost immediately it

was opened, closing behind him as soon as he had entered. Nebamun waited in the street. Huy watched from his corner, praying that no stray servant would come upon him and question him. The wall of the house opposite, as he had expected, was blank. The entrance was therefore not overlooked. There was no shop, no well, not even a shady square at one end of the street.

The mist had dispersed and the rising sun in the *matet* boat cast a shadowless white light. Aware of the noise his sandals made on the gravel, Huy walked away from the corner and found a small patch of shade. Covering his head, he squatted down to wait.

After no more than five minutes, Ankhu emerged and walked back the way he had come, Nebamun falling into step beside him without a word. He no longer carried the parcel wrapped in vine leaves. Huy watched them go. Ankhu's eyes were dark, his jaw clenched in anger.

Huy settled back. Nothing moved and there was no sound. People who were going out would have left by now and no one would return before the sun had passed its high point. The light turned the dusty floor of the street white, and its movement robbed him of the grudging shade. An hour passed, and as if by a signal the crickets started in unison, their monotonous song making him drowsy as small shadows once again began to colonise the street. So quiet was it that a cobra uncoiled itself from some hidden recess and, black against the white, made its unhurried, liquid way down the centre of the street. Another hour went by, and Huy was beginning to wonder if he had been mistaken to stay, if perhaps no one would emerge before night, when the door opened, and a tall, well-dressed man, his head cloaked in a shawl against the sun, emerged and hurried down the street towards the centre of the town.

Huy had recognised Surere immediately, but dressed as he was he would arouse no attention in anyone else. He would soon mingle with the crowd. Huy was pleased that he had thought in the same way as Surere: now was the safest time of day to move around, when people's minds were on their work and their own affairs, when there were plenty of people about, and when heat slowed the senses of all but those who needed to be alert to survive.

As soon as the slender figure had vanished at the end of the street, Huy walked swiftly up to the door and ran his good right hand around it. It was a well-made door, set flush to the wall, and its bolt was so cleverly concealed that Huy could not find it. However it had a wooden handle set in its centre. Huy managed to place one foot on it, and, by reaching up, grasped the upper edge of the lintel above the door, and hauled himself up. Balancing on his feet and the painfully extended fingers of his left hand, he reached up with his right to the shutters of the small window. Sweat poured down his face as he manipulated them, letting out his breath with a rush when he succeeded in opening them. They swung out under their own weight and banged against the wall. Huy held his breath. The noise had been a thunderclap. For long moments he clung there, unwilling to give up his hard-attained position if he could continue to take advantage of it, but afraid that someone would come running. No one did. Laboriously, he got his good hand over the sill, and by pushing himself to the utmost of his height with his feet, he managed to shove and haul himself up and through the window.

He fell on to the wooden floor of the room behind it with a crash, feeling a stab of pain as his injured left arm took his weight. But in a moment he was upright, and had closed the shutters. He recognised the room instantly. Cautiously he made his way across it to the door and listened; but he knew that if there had been servants, or even a dog, they would long since have been aroused. A part of his heart allowed itself to be momentarily amused at his foolhardiness. Then he opened the door.

He was standing on a narrow gallery overlooking a courtyard which was far smaller than the front of the house justified. It had a neat, but neglected air: a dusty palm tree bowed over a stone bench near a small pool which had been allowed to become half empty. There was no sign of life, or even of occupation. Next to the door of the room from which he had just emerged was another, and next to that an inward-facing window. Beyond it, steep steps – all but a ladder – led down to the courtyard.

Huy did not want to spend longer than he had to upstairs. Here, he was trapped, as there would be no question of escaping from the house again by the window he had entered at. Hastily he tried the door of the second room, and found that it yielded. Inside, there was an old bed, which did not appear to be in use, and the usual low table and chair. A brief search revealed nothing, apart from two crumbling rolls of papyrus on which the writing was too faded to be decipherable.

There were no further rooms on this floor: the wall forming the opposite side of the courtyard must have belonged to another house. Downstairs, there were two more rooms. One was an entrance hall. The other contained a bed, a long, low table, and three stools. On two of the stools small, identical wooden chests had been placed. On the table was the package Ankhu had brought. It had been opened. The contents, still neatly packed, glittered in the soft light: agates, amethysts, red and yellow jasper, beryls, carnelians, garnets, lapis lazuli and gold beads. Some were in the form of necklaces, others of earrings; most were loose stones. Taking care not to disturb them, his ears always straining to pick up any sound from the street outside, Huy turned his attention to the two boxes. One was new; the other, Huy now saw, was chafed, and bore traces of sand. It was made of good cedarwood, and its bottom was wet.

Both boxes were fitted with simple bolts, which, however, Huy drew cautiously. Surere would not have been above placing scorpions in the boxes if he had suspected for a moment that they might be tampered with. The new box contained more jewels and gold beads. It was almost full, and Huy could not lift it with one hand. There were no scorpions. The second box contained papers. They were accounts. Each of the five small rolls of papyrus bore tightly-crammed lists of figures, in red and black ink.

Huy scanned their contents swiftly and understood. He also understood why the rolls of paper were new, though their contents covered transactions several years old. They were copies. Surere would have the originals safe somewhere else. He must have secured them as insurance, before his downfall.

Outside, it did not take Huy long to find the recently-dug hole, concealed by a flagstone, in which Surere had hidden the box of papers. He could imagine the transaction by which he presented one little scroll to Ankhu in return for each new delivery of jewels, no doubt promising the return of the originals once he was safely away. In the meantime, Huy imagined, Surere had found a way of financing his mission.

161

ELEVEN

Returning to the room from the courtyard, Huy put everything back exactly as he had found it. He made sure that his knife was close to hand, and walked outside again, seating himself on the stone bench by the pool. For the first time he noticed that it contained two large fish, gasping side by side near the surface, their stupid, greedy faces staring avidly at nothing. Huy looked around for the water storage jar, found it, and with a small wooden bucket he passed his time by refilling the pool to the brim. He hoped the fish would be grateful, and wondered how long a wait he had ahead of him before Surere reappeared. He lay down on the stone bench.

He knew he had slept, for there was a cramp in his neck and the memory of a dream: he had been on the River, on a boat with Aahmes and their children. It was the time of the *Opet* festival, and they had been happy, making their new year vows to each other with no reserve in their eyes or in their hearts. He could still see the sunlight on the water. Now, as he looked around the dark courtyard, rubbing his neck, he realised that he was still alone. He glanced up at the star-crowded sky, calculating the time. By the temperature alone, it must have been well past the sixth hour.

A prescient instinct must have awoken him, for a matter of minutes later the bolt of the door was drawn softly, and Surere slipped into the courtyard. Huy made no attempt to move from his place on the bench, though the stone was cool now and hurt his rump, but the former *nomarch*, his heart turned in on itself, did not notice him immediately. His expression was intent.

As soon as Surere saw him he darted forward, like an animal that does not give warning before it attacks, his hand moving swiftly to his hip for his knife. But Huy already had his out and had stood with equal speed, presenting the side of his body to his adversary, balancing on his toes. For a moment they were still, staring at each other in silence, the world shrunk to the space they stood in. Then Surere smiled.

'So. This time you visit me.'

'Yes.'

'How did you find me?'

'I followed Ankhu. I was surprised to see him. I thought he was gathering a party to hunt you.'

Surere looked thoughtful. 'That is unlikely, but the boy is full of bluster. In any case, as you have discovered, he knows where I am. How long have you been here?'

'Since then.'

'So you have found everything.'

'You hid nothing.'

Surere shrugged. 'It was over.'

'Do you have the original papyri?'

'They are safe.'

'Why did you do this, Surere?'

'It was a way of ensuring my safety, and it became a way of collecting funds for my work. I was reclaiming what rightfully belonged to the Aten.'

'When did this start?'

Surere smiled. 'Many years ago.'

'At the City of the Horizon?'

'Yes.'

'How did you know what Reni was doing?'

Surere spread his hands. 'I had the queen's confidence. She did not understand figures, but perhaps she had an inkling something was wrong. I told her that I would keep an eye on things.'

'But how did you get hold of Reni's accounts?'

'That was easy. He fled the city before its collapse. Many of the great officials thought their slate would be wiped clean with the downfall of the king. I made copies myself, and had them, and the originals, hidden here, in the Southern Capital, shortly before Akhenaten's death. We all knew it was coming.'

'Who hid them for you?'

'Someone I could trust. Amenenopet, that sweet boy.'

'How did you know you would need them?'

Surere smiled again. 'I didn't. But I knew that Reni was treacherous enough to have a good chance of surviving the Fall. I swore that if I ever survived, I would make him pay.'

'I have read your copies. Did Reni believe you still had the originals?'

'He couldn't take risks. He recognised his own work. And it made sense to pay me. If the state had found out, he would have had to return it all. He would have been disgraced; and he would have been exiled from the city. It would have killed him.'

'He could have killed you.'

'There was that risk. But I think he was too frightened. He could not know what I had done with the originals, which he believed destroyed years ago. He could not know what provision I had made.'

'What provision had you made?'

'None. But I knew that God would protect me as I was working for Him.'

'What about Reni's daughters?'

Surere sighed. 'That was a pity. After Nephthys had been killed, I knew I could no longer rely on him. His sadness was beginning to make him reckless. He began to speak of sacrifices to Selkit. She is his guardian goddess.'

Huy's mind raced. The *scorpion* goddess. The goddess of the heat of the sun's rays.

'I told him she would not help. He had taken what belonged to Amun, under orders to render it to Aten. But he kept it for himself.'

Huy remembered the great tax levies imposed on the old religion by Akhenaten shortly before his departure from the Southern Capital for the City of the Horizon. Reni had been heavily involved. All the valuables stored up by the priests of Amun were forfeited, taken to finance the new city and the new cult of the One God. Inevitably, some of the funds went missing in the transition, lost in the paperwork: a caravan of donkeys disappeared in the desert, a bullion barge sunk without trace in the river. With the reversion to the old order, the priests of Amun had clawed almost everything back. But not all.

'If Reni had betrayed me I would have given myself up to Kenamun and bought my life with Reni's false accounts,' said Surere. 'They would have sent me back to the labour camps; but at least I would still have been in this world, to escape again, to do my work for the Aten.'

'Might Reni have guessed your plan?'

'Perhaps. It would not have mattered. It might not even have worked. Reni has ingratiated himself with Kenamun. He has information too, which the priest wouldn't wish to be made public.'

'How do you know?'

'His son told me.'

'Why?'

'He hates his father.'

'Then why did he not betray him?'

'He is too good a son for that.'

'But he knows what material his father has to threaten Kenamun with?'

Surere smiled. He no longer looked mad at all. 'There is a brothel in the palace compound which caters to ... special tastes. Kenamun has such tastes. Reni has an interest in the brothel. When I restore the true faith, I will return here and burn all such places to the ground, with their occupants. There will be such cleansing as this city has never known. If only there were not this delay I would leave tonight – but for the orders of the king.'

Huy watched in amazement as Surere abruptly threw himself down on to the stone bench and succumbed to a racking fit of weeping. There was nothing Huy could do to stop it or to give comfort. Awkwardly, he reached forward and touched Surere's shoulder. It felt strange to him to be on a such a footing with this man. It was as if their pasts belonged to other people. He wondered if his own mind could have weathered what Surere's had been through; the changes it had experienced, after so much confidence and so much power.

The weeping subsided. Huy fetched water for Surere to wash in. While the man was recovering, he searched for food. There was none in the house.

'What are the orders of the king?' he asked, finally.

Surere was eager to tell him. 'He is unlike the man I remember. Our lord was always firm, but he was never cruel. He never let anything get in his way, but he did no injustice to anyone else.'

'What did he say?' persisted Huy gently.

'I am glad you are here tonight. I have been in such perplexity. Every order he has given me I have obeyed: to stay here when I wanted to leave; to collect more and more from Reni even though I had enough. And now this.' Surere lapsed once again into an infuriating, brooding silence.

'Now?' Huy ventured at length. He dared not push too hard; nor was he sure yet whether the king existed anywhere but in Surere's heart.

'He tells me I must say I killed the four girls.'

Huy did not speak at once. He did not know how much Surere knew about the murders; he was not even sure that Surere was not the murderer. This order from the king was unambivalent; but if Surere was guilty, and the king a figment of his heart, then why should he feel that the demand was unjust? But there was another thing. Five girls had died.

'Did you agree?'

'How could I? I have killed no one. If there is need for the innocent of this city to perish, to be spared iniquity, then it is for God to decide. And if God chooses me to be his agent in this, I will know.'

'Are you sure you have not been chosen, perhaps without the conscious knowledge of your heart?'

'How could I have performed the killings? In the palace compound?'

'You have learnt stealth.'

'You will not believe me.'

'You know how many girls have died. Do you know their names?'

'Yes.'

166

'How? Because you watched them? Because you decided they should die?'

Surere looked like a trapped beast. He sucked in his breath. 'I know them because the king told me.'

'When?'

'Tonight.'

'Why I should believe you?'

Surere was still for an instant, then came to a decision. 'You must see the king for yourself. You are a faithful servant. He will welcome you.'

Huy hesitated. Fear, sudden and undeniable, rose in his throat. 'Where do you meet him?'

But Surere was cunning. 'I will show you. And you will not leave me before we go. I do not want you to trap me.'

'I swear I will not.'

'He has told me to come to him again this next night. He says he will bring a confession. I must sign it and then die.' Surere said this with simple regret. 'Perhaps we can dissuade him. I have more important work to do for him. It is not yet my time to die. I will teach the Semites the doctrine of Aten.'

The day that followed was the longest of Huy's life. He discussed the reign of Akhenaten endlessly with Surere, going over and over the last days, the final insanity, the wilful sacrifice of the northern empire. Surere reminisced sentimentally about his last lover, the freed slave Amenenopet, that joyful young man from beyond the Great Green somewhere, with his fair skin and blond, curly hair. How the sun had tormented him at first! Did Huy know what had happened to him? How long it had taken him to get used to his Black Land name! And his laughter – like bells ringing in a strange land. When talk faded, Surere produced a box of *senet*, and they played the game until the sun set, each man feeling the anticipation rise in his stomach with the lengthening of the shadows, and each aware of it in the other. Neither had eaten, and Surere had not mentioned food. There was only water to drink. Huy felt in need of bread and wine, but knew that lack of them sharpened his senses.

He managed to fit veiled questions into the conversation

about the deaths of Merymose and the Twin Rivers girl. Surere showed no interest in either of them, nor did he seem to know anything about them.

The long hours, the stilted conversation, the tension of the approaching night, took their toll on Huy. By contrast, Surere was serene. He constantly spoke of the comfort he derived from Huy's presence, and the pleasure he would take in presenting him to the king.

'Keep in the background at the beginning,' he said. 'I will call you when the moment comes.'

Huy knew then that they would meet no king. He felt the knife resting against his thigh under his kilt. Tomorrow, he would tell Ipuky what he believed. Ipuky would tell Kenamun, and Kenamun would have his murderer. Then, perhaps, Huy would discover what had happened to Merymose, and the Twin Rivers girl, and how their deaths fitted into the puzzle that had thrown out two more strands now.

At last Surere stood up. Suddenly all the hours of waiting seemed too short a time. Fatigue had to be shouldered aside. Huy splashed his face with water and shook out his kilt. His stomach was hollow.

'I am ready.'

Surere had hidden the two boxes, pushing them under the bed in an arbitrary and untidy way which was uncharacteristic but which indicated that his heart was already on other matters. Silently they passed through the door and into the street. There was no moon but the sky dazzled with stars, the old immortal ones, who were there before the gods themselves, and who had looked down on the Black Land even before men, the inventors of God, walked the earth. That had been the teaching of the Aten. Out of what curious animal did we stumble? Huy thought, following Surere's lean back as he led the way down through the streets towards the quay.

Apart from a few watchmen posted on the laden boats, no one was about. Surere made his way north along the river-front until he came to a small wooden jetty ending in a ladder, at the foot of which a small ferry-boat was moored. They climbed aboard and Surere cast off, manoeuvring the little craft into the stream with ease.

Once on the west bank, they made fast to the side of one of the large workmen's barges, and clambered over it on to the land. Above them and to the south, two or three small lights winked from the tents where some of the artisans at work on the tombs were spending the night. Huy and Surere made directly inland before turning north. By now Huy knew where they were going, and was not surprised. Nefertiti's burial chamber lay only a few hundred paces ahead.

'I have been coming here ever since I returned to the Southern Capital,' said Surere. 'Her tomb has been neglected. I have done what I can to clear the rubbish from it, but there is too much work for one man.'

'When did the king appear to you first?'

'It was during the third visit I made. I think that he had been coming here alone for a long time, perhaps since the moment of his own death. He loved her beyond measure.'

The cartouche containing Nefertiti's name had been carefully cleaned, and the sand and brushweed partially cleared away from the entrance; but even in the faint light Huy could see that the paintwork was weathered and dull, and the place had a sad and neglected air. The entrance doors had been broken, no doubt by tomb robbers, who had grown bold in the period of anarchy which had existed here in the last years of Akhenaten's reign.

When they had approached to within ten paces, Surere motioned to a large boulder which lay by the side of the all but obliterated pathway that led to the tomb. Near it was a low mound, roughly oval in shape. It was the kind of grave in which you might bury a pariah-dog.

'I wanted to show you this,' said Surere proudly.

Huy looked at the grave. Even in this light he could see that it was new.

'God brought me back here to do one good deed, at least,' continued Surere tranquilly. 'He thought he was a good servant of the Aten, but he was not. He hated the queen. She could only bring forth daughters. He thought she was a monster, sent by demons to undermine the Aten. A very primitive man. I don't know how I can ever have been close to him.'

'Paheri?'

'Yes. They never caught him. He had come back here, too. But he was hounded by demons himself. I would never have recognised him, I just took him for another harbour beggar, until he called me by name.'

'What? I thought you were enemies.'

'We were.'

'Why didn't he expose you?'

Surere smiled again. 'He was past hatred, and he acknowledged the punishment of God. I was wrong to fear him.'

'What happened?'

'After the king's fall, he escaped to the desert. He took refuge with desert dwellers, but he had already caught the disease by then. They threw him out as soon as they discovered that he was a leper, and he made his way here to beg. In the shadow of his father's house.' Surere paused. 'He wanted one final favour from me. The disease had already eaten his hands and his face, and his feet were so rotten he could barely walk on them. He wanted me to send him to the Fields of Aarru. I brought him up here and killed him, and buried him so that he could sleep under the protection of the queen he had misjudged. I knew she would forgive him. Forgiveness is better than monuments.' He broke off again, listening. 'Now I must prepare myself, for the king is coming.'

Struggling to contain his full heart, Huy crouched by the boulder while the loyal servant approached the last resting place of his adored queen alone. Surere had brought an offering of white bread. He placed it reverently on a copper dish which lay on a small stone table in front of the entrance. He lit the oil lamp next to it, then knelt, head bowed, and waited. As he watched from his hiding place, Huy felt the hair on his neck rise.

The king appeared. He came from nowhere that Huy could see, suddenly standing in front of Surere, part-hidden in the shadow of the tomb. He was dressed in a long robe, and his face was not clearly visible, but there was no mistaking the huge belly, or the broad hips and thighs. Huy's throat was dry, and he prayed that Surere would not call him forward to meet the ghost.

The little scribe could not remember the sound of the king's voice, having only heard it three or four times. When he spoke now, the tone was reedy and high; yet there was something familiar about it. Surere, who had been in the king's presence frequently during his life, accepted it unquestioningly. Huy felt his own soul separate from his body and float above it. But part of his heart held back, and told him: if it is the king, he will know you are here, and you will have no power over what he does. If it is not the king . . .

'Surere!' said Akhenaten.

'My lord.' Surere kept his head bowed, his own voice a whisper.

'I hold out a scroll and a knife. On the scroll is a confession. You will sign it with your Horus-name, with your *nebti*-name, with your Golden-Horus-name, with your *nesu bat*-name, and with your Son-of-Ra-name. Then you will take the knife and fall on it, entering the Boat of the Night to join me in the Fields of Aarru.'

'But what must I confess?' Surere looked up, trembling, his fear of death greater than his fear of Akhenaten. 'Why must I do this?'

'It is not for you to question my word. My word is the word of God. The scroll tells of the children you have sent to me to protect them from evil, and of the Medjay, Merymose, who would have thwarted me.'

Surere bowed his head again, raising his hands to receive the paper and the knife. The king stepped forward to give them to him. As he did so, his face came into the starlight and Huy could see that it was covered by a clay mask in a crude likeness of Akhenaten. Now his heart was sure; but he stayed where he was.

The king placed a scribe's palette, with ink cake, brushes and water bowl, on the table next to the bread and the lamp. As if asleep, Surere unrolled the small scroll and signed his name. Then he took up the knife. Huy moved into the open.

'Have you decided to stop killing?' he asked the king loudly.

The masked head swung round. Surere, with a moan of terror, scuttled into the darkness, still clutching the knife. 'Surere!' Huy shouted after him. 'This is not the king!'

The figure was pulling off its robe, and with it the padding which made up the false stomach and distended hips and thighs. A long dagger had appeared in its hand. Then a hand went up and removed the mask.

The dark eyes held a gloating triumph. The mouth was turned down. The face looked far older than it was.

'No, I have not stopped killing. My work will never stop. But every day you have been getting closer to me, and it was time to pause, to shake you off. Surere has milked Reni enough now, and his usefulness is at an end. It is a pity he brought you here. I had hoped for a tidier conclusion. Think: the four girls, and Merymose. The riddle of their deaths solved by the confession of a madman. Your time would have come later. I already had your trust.'

Under the cold light of the stars, the sand was grey as pearls. Huy shifted his weight, watching the knife.

'Did you really think you could persuade him to kill himself?'

'He believed I was the old king. I followed him here once, after my father organised the hiding place for him in the old town house, and paid the first instalment of his blackmail. Surere disappointed me. I thought he was sincere; I thought he shared my ideas about innocence; but he was corrupt, like all the others. After my sisters' deaths, my wretched brother started to pick up the scent.'

'Why did you kill them?'

'To save them.' Nebamun ripped off the remains of his costume, and stood naked and taut in the sand, the knife solid in his hand. 'I loved Iritnefert, but she wouldn't have me. She wanted more. She wanted other men. I wasn't good enough. I knew she preferred Ankhu, with his drinking and his hunting. So I made a tryst with her – a last appeal. I knew what I would do. It had to be by water, for

172

purification, and then an embrace. I used an embalmer's probe to kill them.'

Huy looked from the youth's face to the hand holding the knife, judging his moment. From the darkness beyond them, he could hear Surere sobbing.

'Then my sister Nefi. Did you know my father took her to the Glory of Set for Kenamun? Oh, she enjoyed it. Kenamun tied her up and tattooed a scorpion on her back. Her idea. The family goddess. My father helped him. Then she and another girl – a little bitch from the Twin Rivers ... Well, you can use your imagination. The Twin Rivers girl disappeared. But not Nefi. She told me all about it. She thought I'd like to do it with her too. So I played along. It was too late to save her, but not to stop the pollution of her spirit. After that, I wondered about women ... I knew Mertseger. She was a friend, she'd known my sisters from childhood. I'd seen her looking at me. I decided to find out if she was like the others; if she would be ready to fall. She was! But I saved her.'

'And your sister Nephthys?'

'Do you think marriage isn't also a violation?'

Huy breathed quietly.

'Then Merymose found out about the blackmail,' continued Nebamun. 'He followed Surere and discovered the house. I followed him. I wasn't sure what he would do but I thought he'd contact you before he went to Kenamun. And you wouldn't have been content with Surere. I knew it would only be a matter of time before you started to pick up other threads.'

'So you wanted to help me in order to watch me?'

'Of course. I am not a fool.'

'And Merymose?'

'That was easy. I trapped him in the stall and buried him in grain. I couldn't have killed him otherwise – he was too strong for me, and I couldn't rely on taking him completely by surprise.'

'And me?'

Nebamun laughed. 'You are a scribe; Merymose was a soldier. My brother trained me·to use a knife. I do not think you will match me. Especially with one arm in a sling.'

'What did you do to the Twin Rivers girl?'

'Nothing. She disappeared. Perhaps Kenamun got too rough for her and she ran away.'

'And your father?' asked Huy, trying to keep the disgust out of his voice.

'He only watched – everything,' replied Nebamun contemptuously. 'He enjoyed watching. He was always going to one brothel or another. Especially to places where his money would get him whatever he wanted. But he has his punishment now.'

Huy had guessed that the talking was planned to lull him. Now, without warning, Nebamun lunged. Huy stepped back fast, but not quickly enough to prevent the knife from slicing through the linen of his sling and opening a shallow wound the length of his injured forearm.

He brought his own knife out and across in a slashing movement which was uncontrolled and foolish, and ought to have missed completely, but caught the side of Nebamun's throat and opened the great reservoir of life there. Blood pumped out in a jet as Nebamun continued his attacking run for ten more paces, only then staggering forward and lying still, blood murmuring in his throat as he died.

Using his mouth and his good hand, Huy managed to retie the sling. His head rang with pain. He stumbled over to the offering table where the lamp still burned by the bread, and sat down on a corner of it, resting his arms on his knees.

Across the valley, he could see the lights of the workers' tents. Nebamun's blood was black on the grey sand. Above, the eternal, distant stars shone, the far gods, who measured changes in eons.

Huy listened to the silence, and became aware that it contained more than Nebamun's death alone. He wanted to call Surere's name, but his voice would not rise above a whisper, so he set off in the direction the sobbing had come from.

He was crouched under the cartouche of Nefertiti, his knees drawn up to his head, ready to return to Geb, a child of earth going back to his father in the position of the unborn. The bronze knife lay by him, hilt and blade dark with blood. Near it lay a dozen small scrolls of papyrus. One was the confession, which Huy took and burned at the lamp. The others were the originals of Reni's accounts, proof of his embezzlement.

Surere was not yet dead. Huy came up to him and made him as comfortable as he could, putting his good arm round his shoulders. He looked up, his eyes wide as a little child's. 'There is no answer, is there?' he said. 'This is the only end of our confusion.' He nestled his head on his knees again and died quietly.

Huy made his way down to the River. Wearily, he untied the ferry-boat and rowed back to the jetty on the east bank. Dawn was close but still he had the river to himself. He remembered that it was a holiday. Today the new king, Tutankhamun, would formally be shorn of his Lock of Youth. Soon, he would take power into his own hands and the uneasy regency of Ay and Horemheb would be at an end. He tied up the boat and made his way home. Later, he would go to Ipuky and make his last report. Ipuky could do with it as he wished. It worried him that the death of Isis was still a mystery, but the gods do not give tidy endings. He thought of her body, eaten by quicklime in the burial pit for the unclaimed dead, and said a prayer for her poor, abused *Ka*.

There was never going to be enough evidence to bring down Kenamun, her most likely killer; but it was possible that Ipuky would have enough information to close down the Glory of Set. Reni, he knew, would be broken by what had happened. It would be for Ipuky to decide what to do with the accounts. Huy wondered how Ipuky would take the news of his own son's death.

For himself, if Ipuky kept his word, he would own the house he now lived in. An element of security would be back in his life. But Huy did not dare hope that the young pharaoh would pardon him – indeed, as a former servant of the Great Criminal he would do well not to gain too much notoriety.

He washed, aware for the first time of how much of Nebamun's blood had splashed on to him, and went to lie down on his bed; but he could not rest. He watched the sky through his window as it turned paler, finally resolving itself into the hard, invariable blue of late spring, and he listened to the excited bustle, different in quality from usual, of the city waking up to a day of celebration. He thought of Taheb, and of what they would say to each other when she returned. He thought of Nebamun's retreat from disappointment and disillusion into madness; of Surere's hopeless ideals; and of the wretched uncertainty of life.

At last, as the first music struck up in the street, lulled by it, he slept.